Also by José María Merino
The Gold of Dreams

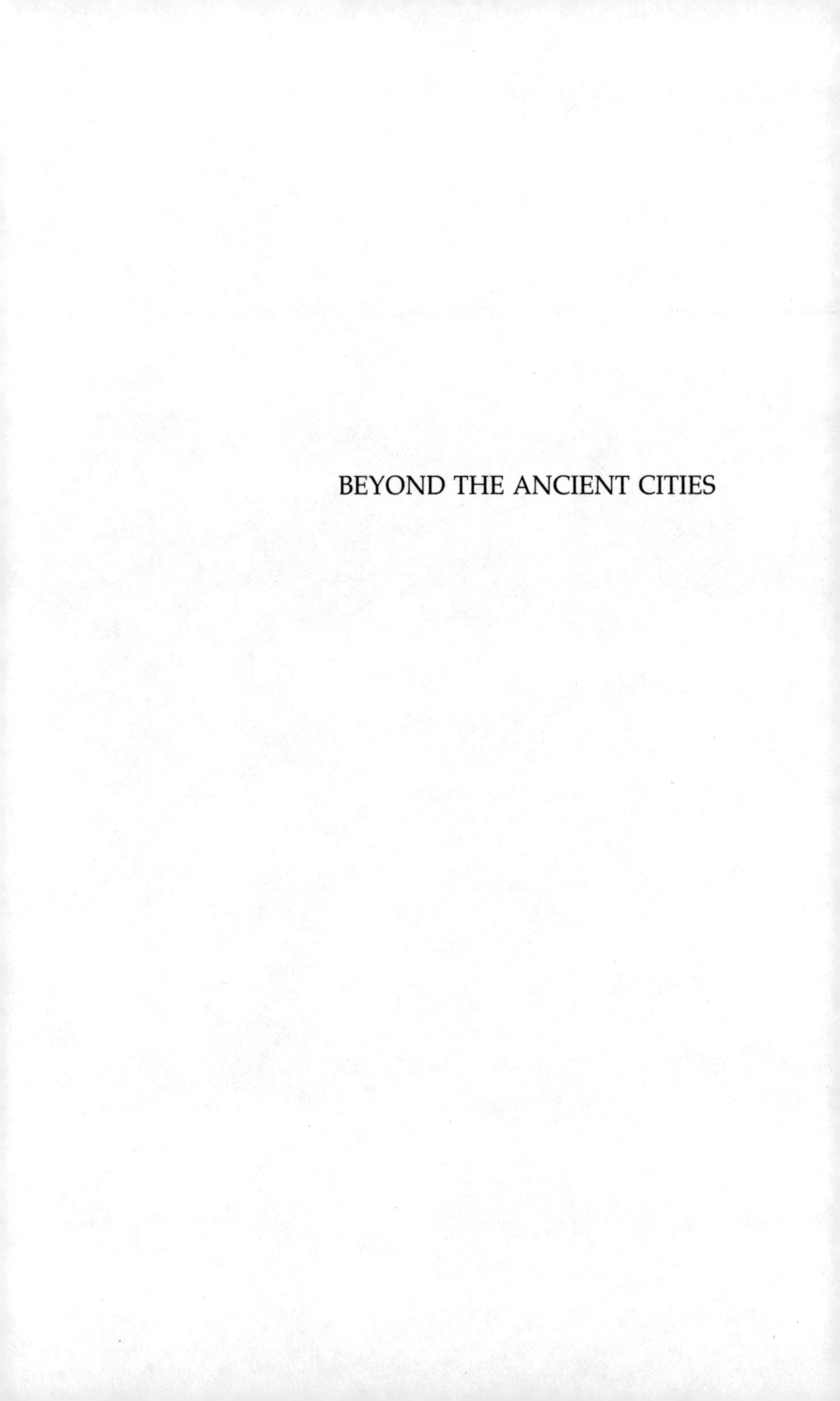

BEYOND THE ANCIENT CITIES

Beyond the Ancient Cities

JOSÉ MARIA MERINO

TRANSLATED BY HELEN LANE

Farrar, Straus and Giroux

New York

Originally published in Spanish by Alfaguara
under the title *La tierra del tiempo perdido*

Published simultaneously in Canada
by HarperCollins*CanadaLtd*
Printed in the United States of America
Designed by Dreu Pennington-McNeil
First edition, 1994

Library of Congress Cataloging-in-Publication Data
Merino, José María.
[Tierra del tiempo perdido. English]
Beyond the ancient cities / José María Merino ; translated by
Helen Lane. — 1st ed.
p. cm.
Companion vol. to: The gold of dreams.
1. America—Discovery and exploration—Spanish—Juvenile fiction.
[1. America—Discovery and exploration—Spanish—Fiction.
2. Mexico—Fiction.] I. Title.
PZ7.M536Be 1994 [Fic]—dc20 93-35482 CIP AC

For Eria

BEYOND THE ANCIENT CITIES

CHAPTER I

I was rummaging about among the weapons and old junk, in the cane shed where the Indians store what they can steal from the soldiers in their skirmishes, when I came across the set of writing materials. They were inside a box of dark wood: an inkwell and a sand sprinkler, several quills, and a leather portfolio with nearly four quires of paper.

I didn't know at first what they were. In the semidarkness, the clinking of the inkwell and the sand sprinkler made me think that I had discovered a set of strange instruments. But some sand fell in my hand, the ink gurgled in the little bottle, and before I got to a spot with more light, I sensed that the objects were similar to those which, on my father's writing desk covered by a velvet cloth, preside over the most revered corner of our family's house.

I remembered the days when I wrote down the account of my first expedition. But an earthquake had buried deep inside the earth those writings of mine, which I'd so carefully hidden in an old cistern; no one will ever read them now. Yet, even though my story will never have a reader, the time when I was setting it down on paper is retained in my mind with a most pleasing and peaceful flavor.

The idea then came to me, in the leisure forced upon me by my godfather's convalescence, of writing down a chronicle of the events that are occurring at this very moment.

It has taken me two days to make up my mind. It was my intention to take one of the quills, cut it, smooth its rough places, hone it to a sharp point, and begin at once to set down, on one of the sheets of paper, the story of my new travails. But those intentions and the pleasant memory of my labors as a writer faded before a great laziness that led me to lie in the shade of a huge silk-cotton tree, with the sun overspreading everything like an endless wave of honey.

Well, I finally resolved to begin, and once again saw how enjoyable a task writing is, when by means of memory turned into words you reconstruct moments you've lived through. Sitting in the shade, leaning over one of the great rectangular stones of the ruins as though it were a writing desk, I set to work very early in the morning. Gentle murmurings can be heard coming from the village, the birds are making a great racket amid the branches, and some children are watching me in silence.

The events in which I am involved in the course of this expedition started on another morning, as High Mass was letting out. It was a cold gray day and people lingered in the portico of the church, casting long glances at the cart of Luengo, the muleteer.

People say that Luengo was a felon who had served a sentence in the galleys, as meted out to him by the King's justice, and then was given license to come to New Spain. Ever since I was a little boy, I've had the same memory of him: a very old, toothless man, always accompanied by an Indian woman, also very old, with her hair in long gray plaits, and wearing a delicately embroidered *huipil*, a sleeveless blouse typical of the region she comes from.

Driving a large four-wheeled cart drawn by a big mule, Luengo visits the village two or three times a year. He usually comes, as he did that day, on the morning of a feast day. When people come out of church, they find in the main square, as though by magic, the big black cart, its wooden planks unfolded to serve as counters and its canvas spread out, and displayed on them lengths of cloth in many colors, ribbons and handkerchiefs, prints of saints and of Our Lady, prayer cards and missals, tapers, votive candles, and all sorts of tools and utensils—from those used for spinning to grub hoes and scythes for working the fields.

Luengo the peddler transports from the coast, and also from México–Tenochtitlán, the merchandise he has received orders for, and other goods as well which have come to Veracruz from Spain and which he offers as the latest thing. He is, then, a muleteer and a peddler and without fail brings news of what is happening in Spain, and in Rome, and all over the Indies.

But that day the cart did not have its side planks unfolded, or its canvas unfurled above it. No bright cloth, no shiny baubles announced the presence of colorful goods for sale. The mule, its head with a sack tied over its ears, was grazing, yoked and motionless; on the driver's seat the old Indian woman, bundled up in a blanket, was also as silent and still as a statue.

Luengo the muleteer hurried past me, asking people something that I was unable to hear. He carried in one hand a bundle wrapped in canvas. My eyes followed him as he made his way through the crowd, and I saw him go over to my godfather and speak to him. My godfather stopped and the two withdrew to the other end of the portico. People were leaving the church and the arcades and finally only the two of them were left in the portico. They stayed there talking, making vague, secretive gestures.

In the bundle the peddler was carrying, among a number of other things, there was a paper folded in two. My godfather broke the seals and began reading intently. I approached them. My godfather finished reading, looked up, surprised, and saw me.

"Miguel!" he exclaimed.

"Is something up?"

He smiled with an air of mystery. "There may be. Come have lunch with me."

Anything new broke into the daily routine with a promise and an echo. I went off at a run to tell my mother that I'd be going to my godfather's for lunch. My mother, my sisters, and Lucía were already in the cart that would take them home.

"Is it on account of that letter?" my mother asked.

"What letter?" I said.

"I saw the peddler hand a letter to your godfather."

I shrugged. She sighed and cracked the whip gently in the air, so the horse would set off.

"May God help us!" I heard her exclaim.

I now know that the message was indeed an omen of adventures to come. But at the time I merely felt it might be. At lunch, my godfather kept my curiosity piqued until dessert. I was impatient to hear the news. The possibility of something happening that would break the routine of my life in the village, the daily Latin classes and other equally monotonous lessons, made me restless. Indeed, my first sally into the world, rather than frightening me with its ill-fated events, had awakened my appetite to roam the four corners of the earth, no matter whether my destiny was to be fortunate or unfortunate, for even though that adventure had been ill-starred for many, it had brought me riches of a sort and good friends.

"Well," my godfather finally said, getting up from the table. "Are you ready to leave those Latin studies of yours for a while and venture forth with me again?"

I answered, stammering: "You know only too well that I am, my lord Godfather."

He had gone over to his desk and picked up the letter.

"Do you remember that gentleman we met in Pánuco who was in the service of His Majesty?"

How could I not remember? He was uncle to someone very close to me, someone who had been with me through many ups and downs of fortune and who had returned to Spain but had not answered my two letters. My interest grew.

My godfather said solemnly: "He has sent me this missive, asking for our help."

My godfather had assumed a martial posture, one hand resting on the baldric of his sword, the other holding the letter, which he waved about as though brandishing a weapon.

"His letter is written from the Court, where they are seeking a way to put a stop to the unruliness in Peru. There is war there, between Spaniards and the Indians in the mountains who have risen in revolt, private justice replacing the King's."

My godfather is not a braggart, nor does he give the appearance of being one. But though he keeps a tight rein on his pride, at times there is a brief and noticeable flare-up of it. "They are requesting my services to offer wise counsel to the new president of the Royal Tribunal of Panama, who is soon to arrive in the Indies and who will be obliged to intervene in what is happening in Peru. They value my proven loyalty to His Majesty our King, my experience in critical moments both trying and glorious, my knowledge of and skill in combat."

He went to his desk once more and picked up a large envelope, which he also waved in the air emphatically. "These are my credentials. It is a post of great honor, as is the recompense. It is also my privilege to appoint anyone I choose to assist me."

I looked with wonder at the envelope sealed with wax bearing the royal impress, and was unable to give any sign of my surprise. My godfather burst out laughing and grabbed me affectionately by the ear.

"In these papers, you are appointed as my secretary. We will be leaving soon. Tell your mother the news and set about getting ready."

When I returned home, on the back of one of his mounts, it was beginning to rain. My mother, my sisters, Lucía, and my old nursemaid, Micaela, were sitting on the wooden porch, spinning and shelling maize. My brother was in my cousins' village. My mother looked at me long and hard. She didn't need to say a word for me to feel that I had to explain.

"They are seeking don Santiago for a highly important service," I said.

She stood there not speaking, looking me in the eyes.

"I am to accompany him," I added. "He has appointed me to be his secretary."

Now they all stared at me.

Old Micaela gestured with her hands. "Mistress," she said in the old language, addressing my mother, "don't be sad. It is this lad's destiny to travel to distant lands. It is a characteristic of the sun, which has come down to him through his father's lineage."

My mother came over and put her arms around me. She, too, spoke in the old language. "When will you be leaving?"

"I don't know yet. But Godfather told me that I should start preparing for the journey."

My news broke up the gathering and I found myself

alone facing the afternoon and the rain, which slid in large drops from the roof. In the branches of a dried-up tree on the boundary of our land, a number of turkey buzzards perched, motionless, like bad omens. Yet I felt happy, already picturing other trees and other birds, as well as other rains, different from the rain that presently concealed the distant horizon behind a wide silver wall.

I have inherited from my Indian mother a great aptitude for dreaming and for serenity; but no doubt my father's Spanish blood sparks my urge to journey afar and discover and know lands unlike my own.

Darkness fell and I went inside. A lamp lit the room. Everyone had withdrawn to one corner and they were all praying in low voices. When I saw the look in the eyes of my sisters and Lucía, I realized that they were praying for me. I felt a sudden flash of remorse. At the same time a bright flash of lightning, close by, followed by a loud clap of thunder crossed the sky of the village, announcing a storm that was to last almost all night.

CHAPTER II

Several days passed and my impatience grew to the point of keeping me awake at night, as time dragged along with the slowest possible steps.

Each afternoon, as soon as I finished my lessons at the monastery, I ran to my godfather's house to find out the latest word concerning our departure. The rains had recently begun and there were heavy downpours, so I often arrived nearly soaked to the skin.

My godfather kept thinking about the best way to reach Panama. The journey overland was dangerous. A number of regions had been conquered by Spaniards—many by don Pedro de Alvarado, my godfather's comrade-in-arms in the conquest of Anahuac—but in other areas that we would have to cross, toward the southwest and

Castilla del Oro, a war of conquest was still raging, and there were no roads or inns or hostelries for travelers.

It was necessary, then, to travel by boat. Luengo the peddler had reported that don Hernando Cortés was setting up a port near his residence, to build ships and to transport cargo and passengers from the shores of Oaxaca, via the Southern Sea, to a remote part of Peru that had recently been conquered and of which so many marvels had been recounted. It appeared, however, that the voyage was a very long one, that the pilots were unfamiliar with the routes, and that vessels were in short supply.

But when I came in that afternoon, my godfather met me with open arms. "It's been decided, Miguel!" he said.

I nearly shouted for joy.

"We will ship out from Veracruz," he continued. "Several friars came through town this morning, and I found out that the same boat that brought them from Santo Domingo will soon be setting sail for Nombre de Dios in Panama."

The rainwater was dripping from my hooded cape and I could feel it running down my legs, but I was so pleased with the news that I paid it little heed.

"Vasco Núñez took off from that very port when he discovered the Southern Sea," my godfather explained. "Panama is only a few leagues away overland and there we will board a ship destined for the port of El Callao in Peru."

He took me by both shoulders and gave me an affectionate shake. "You have two days to get ready. We will leave next Saturday at dawn, God willing. I will come by your house to get you."

I had been awaiting that news so eagerly that without a word, not waiting for the cart to be hitched up to take me back to my village, I turned and ran out into the rain. It was a long way and my heart was pounding in my breast, to the rhythm of my strides. I imagined that, through one of those magic virtues found in fairy tales, I was wearing a pair of fabulous boots that allowed me to cover leagues with each step, and that with the same swiftness I would soon see myself in Veracruz and on the high seas and in the various ports, and then finally in Peru, where the people cover their walls with gold and make their roads out of polished stone.

The dizzying sensation from an accelerated heartbeat stayed with me as I packed my clothes in a large leather traveling bag and my combat equipment in a wooden coffer with sturdy metal fittings.

In the last few months, with the treasure found on my first journey, I had ordered for myself two pairs of sturdy boots, some fine shirts, doublets and several pairs of hose, a hat and a leather jacket. I also ordered a good sword made to my measure, a light, strong crossbow, a helmet, and a steel breastplate. In the two days before my departure, my mother and Micaela fashioned a pair of cotton hauberks similar to the ones that protected my Indian forebears in combat.

My mother and I were putting my paraphernalia in order—she was placing fragrant little sachets between my garments so as to keep insects away—when she said she had to ask me something about Lucía.

"Lucía? What about Lucía?"

"She wants to go with you."

Lucía is of pure Indian stock, but she had lived with Spaniards, on the other side of the ocean, ever since she was a little girl. I had met her on my last journey and at its end she came back home with me, leaving her Spanish mistress's company. During the time that she had lived in our house, I discovered in her a joyousness and a vivaciousness that I hadn't known she possessed.

I was puzzled. "I thought she liked it here."

"That's not the reason, my son. She is happy with us. But she knows that when you reach your destination you are going to need someone to look after you and keep your household in order."

I realized that she approved of Lucía's wish.

"I don't know what Godfather will think," I said.

"I'll speak to him myself, if need be. To my way of thinking, Lucía shows great good sense when she speaks. Moreover, she is obliging and attentive to details. She likes you."

I looked at her without saying a word.

"She'll be of great help to you," she added.

Later, when I told all this to Godfather, he raised no objection whatsoever. "So be it. Let the girl attend to the household tasks. I for my part am going to take along Rubén the black to look after the horses and mules and to be our overseer."

My godfather seemed circumspect, as though his forthcoming mission had given him a different view of himself. He spoke in measured tones, with slow, grave gestures.

"Miguel, my boy," he said. "In Peru, we shall enjoy a public eminence different from what we are accustomed to in these settlements. It is well that we are including within our number the people who can be of service to us in our future way of life."

My euphoria suffered a brief decline on the eve of our departure.

I had already bid farewell to almost everyone: to my teacher—who was no longer that Friar Bernardino, who had taught me since I was a child, for his Order had transferred him elsewhere; to my friends, and to the people of the village. I had joked with my sisters, for the last time, about how rich I was going to be in my new position, and my mother gave me those bits of advice which, having to do with banal, everyday matters, are a clear sign that the time has come to say goodbye.

Among all these farewells, my grandfather's had proved to be particularly moving. He received me in his oratory and recited, for my safety, the prayers and petitions of his cult. He warned me never to remove from around my neck the slender chain from which hung a tiny gold hummingbird. He had given it to me before my last journey, as a token of good luck. I found him very slow-witted, with a greater number of wrinkles, and his usually hoarse voice was even more feeble because of his intermittent fainting spells. I realized that in all probability I would never see him again.

I left his room and headed toward one of the sheds to get a lantern that I needed for the journey. All of a sudden, my taste for traveling was dimmed by a feeling of loneliness. It was not raining, but the afternoon was overcast. My joy in leaving had also been darkened by the sense I had that I was going away forever. It was a feeling that the sight of the house where I was born, and the garden, the rows of stables and the henhouses, the entire vista of gray, green, and ocher colors beneath the murky sky, where at that moment not a single human figure was to be seen, was presenting itself to my gaze for the last time.

I shook my head, went into the shed, searched for the lantern, and returned home at a rapid pace, doing my best, by the resoluteness of my movements, to exorcise the traps of doubt that lay hidden in my mind.

My mother was putting the last of my garments in the traveling bag. She stroked my hair the way she used to when I was a little boy. "Miguel," she said. "You must do as I bid you."

I burst out laughing. "I always do as you bid me, Mother."

Her face had not lost its protective look, but she shook her head in a gesture of gentle reproach.

"What would you like me to do?" I asked.

She picked up a small object and handed it to me: a wrinkled leather pouch that I recognized immediately.

"You are to take this with you," she said.

It was the great emerald, resembling a polished sphere, that I had brought back for her from my first adventure. Looking at the stone brought back any number of bitter memories.

"You are heading off to distant lands. Calamities may befall you."

"I'm taking a goodly amount of gold with me. Godfather is, too. And he says that our pay will be most generous."

"Hide it carefully away within your clothes," she went on, paying no attention to what I had just said. "These are dangerous times."

"But you, too, may fall on hard times," I said.

"We have our land, our animals. We won't lack for anything to eat or to wear."

I did not want to go against her wishes. But the emerald upset me in a strange way. I was afraid of it. To my way of thinking, its influence on the lives of all of us had been ill-fated. I had a strong intuition against accepting it; only if it remained in my mother's hands would the curse it might bear be exorcised.

"No, Mother," I said in a firm voice. "I am not going to take it with me. Forgive me."

She did not press the point and went off with the pouch. The clouds in my mind evaporated and, despite having gone against my mother's wishes, I felt abounding joy at the sight of the bundles of my clothes and equipment.

CHAPTER III

It was still dark when my godfather arrived, but I had already harnessed my mule and loaded my equipment onto the cart. My mother was at my side, and my sisters watched us from the porch railing with sleepy eyes. Micaela was close by, too, looking tearful. "The cocks aren't crowing today," she lamented, between doleful murmurs, a certain sign that to her boded ill.

I embraced my mother. A faint light was dawning in the east. All of a sudden a long, deafening cock-a-doodle-doo sounded. I mounted the mule and said jokingly: "They're crowing now, Micaela, there's no doubt about it."

My godfather, who was also astride his mount, waved the hat he was holding in his right hand. The big multicolored plume gleamed in the half-light.

"Goodbye, my good doña Teresa. Farewell to one and all."

Although hidden by clouds, the sky took on a pale coloring. Rubén was holding the reins of the cart and Lucía was sitting alongside him. I went ahead on my mule at a brisk trot, so as to leave behind me as quickly as possible my house and the gaze of my family. I was ashamed at finding myself in such a happy, expectant mood while their faces expressed such obvious sorrow. I finally halted at the top of the slope and waited for the cart to catch up. A reddish ray from the rising sun reflected off the crests of the volcanoes. As I looked back, my village was calm and silent; the tiny shapes of the villagers began to disappear among the houses.

As we went through the hamlet, we ran into Luengo the peddler, who was also setting out on his travels. Our route would be the same for quite a few leagues, so we decided to share that part of the journey. A skinny dog trotted alongside Luengo's cart and every so often the peddler addressed it in unintelligible phrases.

The sun never did succeed in driving the clouds away, but neither did it rain. Then we descended to the plains, where the weather was neither hot nor rainy, but very pleasant. I was riding near Luengo when he abandoned the undecipherable messages jabbered at his dog and spoke to me. I didn't hear him the first time and he leaned out of the cart toward me.

"You're in a very happy mood, my boy," he said in a clear voice.

Without being aware of it, as though my mind wished to prove of its own volition how joyous the journey was making me feel, I had been riding along humming little songs and ballads.

"And why shouldn't I be?" I retorted after an instant.

"At your age, any change made me happy, too," he said. "I arrived in the islands when I was fifteen, and I thought I was in the earthly paradise."

His missing teeth filled his voice with soft whistles.

"But paradise is no longer to be found in this world," he added.

"This isn't the first time I've left home," I said. "I participated in don Pedro de Rueda's invasions of the kingdoms of Yupaha." I wanted to show him that I wasn't a greenhorn.

"I know all about that disaster," he replied, clacking his tongue loudly. "More than two hundred of you began the expedition, and only ten came back alive."

"Eight," I muttered.

"So then you know from experience what I mean. When I arrived in the Indies, I thought I was in Eden itself. The Indians were friendly and hospitable. But on my ship were people taken ill with fever—some sort of sickness that was hardly fatal to a Christian, but it was a catastrophe for the Indians, almost all of whom died from the disease. It was there that I witnessed for the first time the havoc brought about by death on a vast scale."

I had always thought that Luengo the peddler was closemouthed to the point of surliness and that he spoke only as required for his commercial activities. But he turned out to be loquacious and friendly, and throughout our two days' travel together, he recounted to me many of his adventures in the islands and on Terra Firma.

His memories were generally tinged with a certain skeptical and disillusioned aftertaste. While still very young, he signed on as partner to a scribe to run several farms using forced Indian labor. The undertaking apparently turned out very badly, with enmities between the partners which, although he did not explain them to me in detail, must have been very serious. He also had major problems with the Indians. They detested the work to which they were bound by royal decree to perform for Spanish colonists under the encomienda system, to the point that many of them preferred to take their own lives.

"It wasn't the work," I asserted. "It was the new way of life. They need their traditions. I know them well."

But he wasn't listening to me.

"One of my overseers prevented some of the Indians from committing suicide by telling them that he would hang himself, too, since if they killed themselves, thus abandoning their labors, it would be the ruin of them all. They were people of a fundamentally good nature; it gave every appearance of having existed long before Original Sin. Later I came to know others who were worse than wild beasts."

I gathered that his association with his partner ended dramatically, an ending that had brought him before the bar of justice, because he showed me a long scar on his arm that, according to him, had come from a knife wound inflicted by his partner.

"He paid dearly for it. And so did I."

He was rumored to have been sentenced to the galleys, which may have been the payment he was speaking of, but he never went on to tell me the whole story. He spoke of expeditions as full of the kind of hardships that I had experienced the first time I sallied forth into the world. But he had heard of even more terrible events, expeditions in which the handful of survivors had to resort to cannibalism, or others still in which not one soul came back alive.

"In an invasion in the region of Darien," he continued, "we were following the trail of previous discoverers, marked by the remains of their camps and by a succession of corpses, each more hastily and less carefully buried than the one before. The trail ended in some hills, between huge spheres of carved stone and idols with hideous faces. The skeletons of Indians and of Christians were scattered about everywhere. Not a one had managed to survive starvation, their wounds, and the predators. On a bit of parchment, the field commander had written down the account of the final part of that undertaking."

The mule was so accustomed to being driven that Luengo left the reins tied to one side of the driver's seat, commanding it with clacks of his tongue. As for his wife, he said very little to her, and when he did, it was in a low voice, and in the old language. I noticed that she never wasted a single moment: she embroidered, knitted, or was always preparing tortillas and other food, squatting down or kneeling in the cart as though on the floor of an Indian hut, paying no heed to the swaying back and forth caused by the rough road, which was more a path for pack animals than a road suitable for wheeled vehicles. Every so often, both Luengo and his wife lighted up a dark tube as broad as a person's thumb and perhaps as long as the span of a hand, and raised it to their mouths as though they were drinking in some sort of scented smoke.

The first night we slept in the shelter of the carts, by a small pond. The second night we stayed at an inn that had just opened, at a junction with the new road to México–Tenochtitlán. The inn was a large stone building, with a square patio overlooked by a balcony on the second floor, where the rooms were. There were stables in the back. Only the roof woven with greenery was like that of the traditional structures of the region.

There was food for us and drinking troughs and fodder for the animals. The peddler drank half a liter of wine from Spain at the invitation of my godfather.

"I offer a toast to the health of so noble a gentleman, to the prosperity of his undertaking, and to the well-being of his entire company. Here's to a happy outcome," said Luengo.

But when we were alone, he said to me: "Everything is an adventure, my lad. Every moment of your life is one, if you know how to recognize its surprises and its treasures, too. There have been endless risks taken by countless people, and there have been countless deaths and failures. Gold is an industry that anyone can engage in, by using his own talents and skills, without having to go off and snatch it from some far-distant ruler."

I objected to this: it was not the usual view of adventures, according to books as renowned as the ones about don Amadís and the exploits of Esplandián, or about don Florisando, or don Palmerín de Oliva, not to mention don Felixmarte de Hircania and don Belianís of Greece.

"They say that His Majesty has forbidden such books to be brought to the Indies and he could never have made a more praiseworthy decision," he said. "Such reading is responsible for the drying up of many honest and reasonable brains and the proliferation of so many chimerical kingdoms."

"Wasn't Moctezuma's empire real?" I asked. "And was there no truth to the reports of an empire called Incario with walls covered with gold?"

"I don't know," he replied, doubtfully. "At my age I believe more strongly in these colored kerchiefs that I sell than in all the treasures of the Indies. I have seen so many acts of sheer madness committed in the name of those kingdoms and their riches that I sometimes wonder whether those very empires that I believed I was well acquainted with might not also have been tricks of extraordinary illusion."

A faint, querulous voice reached our ears. "Don't listen to him, my boy," it went. "Be on your guard against what he's talking about."

The voice belonged to a very young man, bearded, pale, and skinny, with a blanket over his shoulders. He was sitting by the door to the patio. The peddler gave him a hostile look.

The young man, making an obvious effort, went on. "Such things do not exist only in the imaginations of the authors of books. From a mountaintop I have seen on the horizon the first dense vegetation of the cinnamon province, a land where the cinnamon trees grow almost on top of each other over vast expanses, like grain in an immense wheat field. And persons whom I believe implicitly because they have firsthand knowledge have spoken to me of the indomitable Amazons who fiercely defend their mysterious kingdom. And there is a prince in the heart of a certain jungle who, covered with powdered gold, bathes in a hidden lake on the feast days of his cult. The Indies have every surprise and every treasure in store for those with faith and daring."

His voice was weak and hoarse. "I fell ill from what they call sleeping sickness, malignant fevers that have left me in this state, but once I recover I'll go back, for there is no falsehood in what my sources recount. I have seen with my own eyes the gold beams of the Temple of the Sun, and the golden sun that presides over the most sacred site in the Inca empire."

We heard later that the young soldier would be given over to the care of a monastery where a relative of his was the abbot; only his youth had kept alive in him the embers of life.

"He's going there to die, though he doesn't know it," explained a soldier who was accompanying him, in a sad tone of voice.

At which Luengo the peddler, giving a snort of disgust, remarked: "It's people like that who are the real treasure of the Indies."

CHAPTER IV

As is only natural in the course of a journey there were many meetings and departures. On the following day, Luengo the peddler went on his way, once again taking up his unintelligible exhortations to his dog. We, too, went on our own way, with a different destination. Soon forgotten was the image of the dying, fever-ridden soldier who hoped to get well and go in search of some wondrous empire.

The heat of the coast was coming closer and closer, and a torrid sun beat down on the stony ground.

My godfather and I traveled side by side. At times, he would take the credentials of his post out of his leather pouch and contemplate them with rapture.

"If my poor mother could only have known!" he said with a sigh. "For, as you doubtless know, my mission entitles me to the same terms of address as Their Excellencies the bishops."

I wanted to know in detail what his duties would be to the president of the Royal Tribunal, but I finally realized that he himself did not have a very clear idea of what his work was going to consist of. I wondered if he would have difficulty adjusting to undertakings that had nothing to do with arms, since my godfather's life, after his youth as a farmhand, had been entirely spent as a soldier and a warrior engaged in combat.

He turned the conversation away from my questions toward a discussion of our future residence, with its chapel and pleasure gardens and vast reception rooms, as well as the number of servants and attendants that would be at our beck and call, and the need to count on good mounts and a suitable carriage.

In my imagination, our future residence seemed almost like a palace capable of accommodating the feasts and solemnities that my godfather considered necessary to the way of life of a person appointed to his new rank. A multitude of servants would look after our cuisine and would devote themselves to taking personal care of us.

"If we were in one of the provinces of Spain, a band of minstrels would also be at our service; they would play their instruments as we had our midday meal, or for the enjoyment of our guests. But in Peru there is a shortage of musicians of merit," he said.

I also wanted to know what my obligations as his secretary would be. He was silent for a time and then spoke to me in the tone of voice which seemingly would correspond to his new status: "You will be assigned an amanuensis whose job will be to take care of everything. Seeing that he does his work will be your one and only responsibility."

Then his tone of voice changed. "Don't let anything worry you, Miguel. We will be giving the orders, and others will carry them out. For, as the proverbial wise man once said, the person in command must look after his own interests first of all, do little, and do it very slowly."

Eventually we reached the Villa Rica de la Vera Cruz. In the short time that had gone by since I first became acquainted with it, the town had grown in size, and we could see a number of buildings under construction. The heat slathered our bodies with its damp stickiness. The air was stifling and sultry.

We headed for the inn of San Juan, where we had stayed for a night on our previous journey. On the wall in the dining room, in a place of honor, hung the same blackened guitar which someone now far away, whom I will always remember with affection, used to accompany ballads and popular songs.

The innkeeper embraced my godfather joyfully. They had been comrades in arms in the wars of conquest. But their initial happiness soon gave way to anxiety. For, according to what that potbellied, profusely sweating man, who often voiced his hatred of the bad weather of Veracruz, told us, the flotilla headed for Panama, which had brought the friars from Santo Domingo, had instead left for Havana. At that time of year he thought it unlikely that any other ship able to go on to Nombre de Dios would come into port in the next three or four months.

"But we must get to Panama as soon as possible."

The innkeeper, wiping his sweat with a big handkerchief, looked glum and shook his head dubiously.

However, after several days of discouragement and humidity from a heat wave that kept getting worse and worse, and as the notables of the city began to abandon it, as was their habit, to escape its bad climate for the next few months, we heard news that a ship had in fact arrived. My godfather, Lucía, and I headed down to the port immediately.

It was an odd-colored caravel. We could see at once that the color was due to a lack of paint, for it was the most neglected, battered ship that I've ever set eyes on. Its filthiness and slovenly appearance were evident not only on the hull but also in the rigging, the masts and yards, the sails, and even the crow's nest. Some of the seamen, also slovenly and dirty, looked on lazily as a handful of Indians unloaded cargo onto the dock.

My godfather found out that the ship would be going on to Santo Domingo to deliver cargo there, too. He asked to speak with the captain or master of the vessel, but he was told that he was resting just then. Finally, the boatswain disembarked; a skinny, ungainly man with a long red nose, he was dressed in dark, heavy garments that appeared not to be suffocating him, despite the intense heat.

My godfather explained that it was imperative for us to continue our journey. The man listened calmly and distractedly; then there began between the two of them a heated discussion concerning the estimated cargo fees.

Lucía and I went wandering about the port. The Indian children were taking a swim, shouting playfully, at the foot of the wooden pylons. The scene reminded me of the good times I'd had with my playmates, in the pools of the river that bordered my village. I mentioned those days to Lucía, who was in a good mood, though full of my godfather's fantasies concerning the grandeur of our future life.

She said we would need to set up a room in our new residence to serve as a library, where I could go on with my lessons, time permitting. I looked at her in astonishment, as she asserted with a resolute air that no amount of instruction was too great for a person with as much responsibility as me, since I was no doubt destined to hold very high posts.

When we returned to the ship, the captain had joined in on the discussion that my godfather and the boatswain were having. He was quite different in appearance from the boatswain: short, with broad arms and legs, pale-faced, beetlebrowed; he had an air of being self-absorbed and unsociable.

Their conversation lasted for a longer time still, but when they bade each other goodbye the deal concerning the cargo fees had been closed. My godfather gave signs, in equal proportion, of satisfaction for persuading them to change the ship's planned course and annoyance at what in his judgment was an exorbitant price: nearly four hundred solid-gold pesos, which included passage for the three of us and transport charges for our three mounts and our equipment.

The ship's departure was imminent, depending only on how long it took to load the commercial cargo. We passengers were to busy ourselves gathering and getting ready all the supplies necessary for feeding and lodging ourselves properly during the voyage.

Here Lucía gave evidence of her excellent talents as an organizer and a tradeswoman, as though she were not a girl my age but a veteran mess officer who had never done anything else in her life. She was so accurate in her estimate of our needs and the supply of victuals was so varied and well calculated that, had it not been for the lamentable events that would take place on the ship, we would have had ample, even surplus, stores.

First she estimated the time it would take us to reach Nombre de Dios, discussing the matter with a number of people and taking into consideration the time of year. Then she made a lengthy list of possible food supplies and scoured the town in search of those who would provide the best quality at the best price.

She bought jerked beef, fish and salt pork, ship's biscuits made of white flour, and various dried vegetables, as well as fresh onions, garlic, and a number of laying hens. She bought a Spanish wine for Godfather and me of such quality that it tasted as though it had just been brought up from the wine cellar. Apparently, neither the voyage across the ocean nor the intense heat of Veracruz had spoiled it. As for water, even though supplying it was the boatswain's responsibility, she preferred to bring along a few casks of it as well, foresight that was our salvation, as I shall show later on.

CHAPTER V

The ship went on loading its transport: textiles and blankets, cochineal dye, salt, delicate pottery . . . Finally, one day at noon we left the inn to settle ourselves on board; it had been arranged that we would set sail that afternoon, with the turning of the tide. Our equipment and our mounts were loaded, and the innkeeper, to whom Lucía had managed to sell the cart, called out repeated goodbyes to us.

The first thing we noticed on boarding the ship was a terrible odor. The ship was very old—the seamen said that it dated back to the days when don Christopher Columbus discovered the Indies—and the water that had accumulated in the bilge was stagnant, giving off a nearly intolerable stench made worse by the intense heat. The crew consisted of scarcely a dozen men, which my godfather deemed a scanty number, far fewer hands than needed to handle such a ship, which, by his estimate, had a displacement of well over a hundred tons.

They assigned us quarters under the poop deck, and we divided the space into several rooms by means of bundles of equipment and lengths of canvas which served as curtains.

Close by, the pilot was studying his charts. He was a slight man, a redhead, not very talkative, and showed no desire to communicate with us.

Finally, anchors raised and with the bow pointed to the high seas, the ship set out with sails unfurled, leaving behind Veracruz and the small offshore islands that also serve as ports. Although I enjoy sea voyages, my godfather does not. That morning we had attended Mass and taken Communion, as a good omen for our crossing. While Rubén organized the space that was to serve us as a cabin, my godfather crossed himself solemnly and said the Credo to further ensure the good fortune of the voyage.

Then he took a deep breath and said: "May the Almighty watch over our safety and may the labors and hardships that our bodies are about to endure at sea be dedicated to His glory. Amen."

But the journey began with a calm sea and a gentle, favorable breeze that made our progress serene and pleasant. We ate our dinner, unrolled our beds, and lay down. After a while, I heard my godfather and Rubén breathing deeply. As for Lucía, she, too, had lain down in her corner, behind a large trunk.

Then it seemed to me that I heard a sort of babbling, like the sound of strange, soft laughter, coming from overhead on the poop deck, where the captain's cabin was located. The laughter, which went on for a few moments, ended with a sound similar to a dog's bark. Successive dull thumps, like footsteps, came from overhead.

I sat up and looked at the pilot, who was leaning over the compass box, in the light of a small lantern. Alongside him, a sailor was getting ready to take the watch. Neither appeared to be disturbed by the sounds, and the pilot, once he had checked our course and set in place the hourglass which marked the beginning of the next watch, lay down on the other side of the deck, between two large black leather traveling bags.

I dozed off for a time, but the dull thuds overhead and the strange sounds, like laughter or gentle barks, woke me up. I heard a door open and then quick footsteps that echoed the length of a brief run, ending with the unmistakable sound of a body falling into water.

As the splashing went on, I realized that it was not coming from either side of the ship, but from up above, over the roof of our quarters, somewhere above the timberwork of the poop deck.

The small lantern shed a feeble light on the far end of the stern, where the sailor on watch was dozing, with both arms holding on to the tiller. On the other side, the mainmast and the rest of the deck were clearly visible in the moonlight.

I got up from my bedding and carefully climbed the ladder. No longer muffled by the poop deck, the splashing sounds grew more distinct. The unfurled sails occasionally obscured my view, but I could clearly see in the middle of the deck an enormous wooden tub full of water and someone bathing in it amid elated splashes. The silvery moonlight gleamed on a large, smooth white body, on which I thought I detected feminine features.

I was gazing on this curious scene when someone whispered in my ear, giving me such a start that I almost fell off the ladder. It was the boatswain.

"Have you ever seen anything like that, my boy?" he said. "Have you ever seen such beauty?"

He did not wait for my answer. "Our captain caught it. They say that such creatures are fantasies, but you can see her there before your eyes. The daughter of a muse and of a river god, with her golden hair and breasts the color of mother-of-pearl. It is understandable that the captain has lost his head over her."

No matter how long I looked, I was unable to discover in that shining body the attributes that the boatswain praised with such admiration.

"But what is it?" I asked. "What is it?"

He looked at me with his eyes open wide. The moon cast its light on his corneas, giving him a demented expression. "Don't you know, my boy? Don't you see those alabaster arms, that extraordinarily beautiful body, those long, full tresses? Haven't you ever heard tell of sirens?"

The door of the poop-deck cabin opened with a creak. A halo of lantern light outlined the captain's silhouette as he mumbled an unintelligible word. The body frisking about in the tub fell motionless. Then it went around the tub one last time, spattered a fan of water, and jumped out. It leaned on its back, arms alongside the torso, which was erect. A beam of moonlight illuminated the face and was also reflected in the eyes.

But this could not be called a female body. There were no long tresses, nor were there alabaster limbs. It was not a human being. It was an animal with bulging eyes and thick lips bristling with coarse hairs, and a body covered with delicate, close-fitting skin. I had seen quite a few such creatures on small offshore islands, and on sand banks in the deltas of great rivers, on my previous expedition. The thing that made this one different was the color of its skin, as white as milk.

Coming forward with a grotesque, successive clapping of its fins, the creature went into the captain's cabin. Then the boatswain called out to the captain in a low, intense voice. The captain made his way slowly to where we were standing. He did not seem to notice my presence.

"What's the trouble?"

"Captain," the boatswain asked, "what is she telling you? What is she talking to you about?"

The captain's face was a blank slate.

"They are not things that should be made public," he said. "She is as ancient as she is beautiful. She has heard the incomparable singing of Orpheus, who enthralled the monsters of Tartarus and the gods of hell with his lyre, so as to get his wife Eurydice back. As for her own singing, it was heard by Ulysses himself, lashed to the mast by his men. She knows the secrets of the sea and where each and every sunken treasure lies."

He turned to leave.

"Captain, Captain," the boatswain went on. "Aren't you afraid that she'll devour you?"

The captain stopped, hesitated for a few seconds, and then strode swiftly to his cabin and closed the door with a bang.

CHAPTER VI

Night after night, the gurgles and snorts resounded throughout our quarters under the poop deck. During the day, the crewmen changed the water in the huge tub, hauling it out of the sea in buckets. They also filled a large basket with sargasso and seaweed which they drew in with long boat hooks. The basket was then placed near the tub, as though it was the great creature's manger.

I told my godfather what I had seen and remarked that in my opinion both the captain and the boatswain seemed to be caught up in an impossible fantasy.

My godfather worriedly tugged on his beard. The neglected state of the ship was evident both inside and out, and the shorthanded crew seemed indifferent to it. Lucía—who prepared our daily victuals on the cook-stove—commented disgustedly on the carelessness and the downright filthiness of the ship's cook. At night, the men on watch conducted themselves in a most undisciplined way, and everyday tasks were performed slowly and clumsily.

"Luck doesn't seem to be with us when we journey by sea," my godfather said.

He recalled our sea voyage to the kingdoms of Yupaha, a voyage that abounded in dead calms, violent storms, and shipwrecks. But as far as time was concerned, on this voyage we were doing well, as a gentle, damp wind drove us steadily onward, the one disadvantage being the frequent rainsqualls that it brought.

We found out that, despite his general negligence, the captain—who was the owner of the ship as well—was very generous when it came to the sailors' pay. Perhaps his generosity explained why the crew accepted being shorthanded without complaint, though they were obliged to do double duty and more. Not to mention the bad food and the state of neglect into which the caravel had fallen.

Eventually, the persistent dampness had disastrous effects on the ship and on our adventure. The problem was first signaled by an increase in the water in the bilge. The sailors and Rubén took turns working the bilge pumps, which spewed out a brownish water whose fetid odor betrayed the cause of the stench that enveloped the ship.

The pumping had to be done more and more frequently until it was done continuously. Despite the fact that the men never stopped pumping, water began to flood the hold. The sailors explained that even though the hull had not sprung a leak and was indeed miraculously free of shipworm, it had long been in need of careening and caulking, and was now soaked through like a rotten log. A great deal of the tar and oakum that originally stopped up the gaps between the planks had been lost or had not been applied in the right quantities, so water was leaking in through thousands of tiny breeches.

The cargo of blankets in the hold, once they got soaking wet, increased the ship's weight. It was the same with the straw that had been wrapped around the pottery. The increase in weight reduced the speed of the vessel, which, despite the favorable wind, made less headway. To make matters worse, at that point the wind died down and the squalls grew stronger.

When the water in the hold reached the hoofs of our mounts, my godfather forced the crew to hoist them up on deck. We also brought up all of our food supplies and casks of water. The deck was strewn with a miscellaneous collection of bundles of cargo, animals, and people that made maneuvers on board difficult, and the crew stopped working the bilge pumps.

The persistent rain made it impossible to light the cook-stove, so we were forced to eat the food put up in jars. It was then that we realized the fine job that Lucía had done in seeing to it that our supplies would sustain us, for our reserve stores were varied and of good quality, and the water from our casks clean and abundant. This was not true of the crew's provisions, much of which had spoiled. The seamen began to fish for their food, and fortunately there was no lack of fish to be caught. To assuage their thirst, they used buckets to catch the rainwater that ran down the sails, for the fresh water in their casks was no longer fit to drink.

It became hard not to notice that the sailors' habitual indifference was turning into a barely concealed fury. They frequently cursed, and on one occasion two of the crew were on the point of attacking each other with knives, and only Godfather's intervention calmed them down.

The ship kept sinking lower and lower in the water, until the entire hull was submerged. The water rose to the level of the hatchway to the fore of the mainmast that is ordinarily used to load and unload cargo. No one could think how the ship would keep from foundering. The many empty casks in the hold were the only possible explanation of why the hull remained afloat.

One morning my godfather had a word with the boatswain, after which the four of us, along with our three mounts, occupied the forecastle deck. The bow and the stern had begun to be separated by a wide pool of water, and the shape of the ship could only be discerned from the gunwale, which, projecting above the flooded deck, traced its outline. To me, the sight of water all around us reminded me of the old legends handed down from when the Spaniards first arrived in the Indies, about ships that were thought to be strange floating islands.

Despite the rain—from which we managed to protect ourselves with leftover canvas—we had food and water, and even fodder for our mounts. But on the foredeck, on the isolated forecastle, where the crew crowded together for shelter in between their shipboard tasks, the problems were severe.

Though they had found a way to control the rudder by means of a system of planks and braces that extended it to the very end of the poop, keeping the vessel on course was extremely difficult. In addition, for some reason—perhaps, as Lucía suggested, because of the increase in the salinity of the water surrounding the ship as a consequence of the leaking of the cargo of salt—the fish were fleeing, and the crew began to experience hunger.

To add to our troubles, the wind, which had grown stronger, drove the clouds away and there was no more rainwater trickling down the damp sails. We gave the crew one of our casks of water, but their rations were meager and they showed their distress in brusque gestures and bitter voices.

Early one morning, as dawn was breaking, someone shouted, "Sound the alarm! Sound the alarm! A man is making off with the lifeboat!"

In the gleam of the early light, we caught sight of a small triangular sail as it slowly drew away from the ship. Despite the dimness of the light, we made out the pilot's slender form and head of red hair.

"It's the pilot!" the crew shouted. "The pilot is making off with the lifeboat!"

The boatswain shouted insults in a thundering voice: "Ordóñez, you great traitor, you disloyal wretch!"

Then he turned and his shouts became more urgent: "Load the falconet! Get the powder and the cannonballs for the falconet!"

The crew got the heavy cannonballs and a wick, and someone brought a blunderbuss. But there was so much confusion that when they finally managed to get off the first shot, the lifeboat was too far out of range. It seemed to be moving at a fast clip, driven by the most favorable of winds, and the rising sun shone on its sail. I smelled the gunpowder, an odor so characteristic of armed combat. But instead of bringing back memories of victory, it brought to mind the distressing taste of loss.

From the weather deck, the crew helplessly watched the lifeboat drawing farther and farther away. Then the door of the captain's cabin opened and the captain stepped out. "What's the meaning of all this commotion?" he shouted.

For a moment, the crew fell silent. Then all at once they found in the captain the obvious target for their desperation and fury. Yelling wildly, they rushed down the ladders and surrounded him. What they were yelling was unintelligible, but the chorus of voices boded ill.

"What's going on?" the captain shouted again.

A voice made itself heard above the uproar: "The pilot has taken off with the lifeboat and the last of our rations."

Then a grunting sound came from the captain's cabin. The creature, with its long slender torso, bulging eyes, and thick, hairy lips, peeked out the door. It had not come out to take a dip in the tub since the seamen had occupied the poop deck.

"There's your lunch, men!" one of the crew called out.

Whereupon the boatswain gave a shout, with the same harshness as when he saw the pilot fleeing: "Shut your mouths, all of you!"

He had the blunderbuss propped up on the railing. It is a firearm with a very wide mouth, the kind that causes great bloodshed when a ship is boarded by force.

The crew watched him. He had the blunderbuss trained in their direction.

"Captain," he said, "come with me."

The captain stepped away from the crowd of sailors, and the two men, after prodding the animal back inside the cabin, went in, too, and closed the door behind them. The crewmen burst out cursing.

"Miguel, my boy," Godfather spoke softly behind me, "let us prepare for what is about to happen." He pointed to the large bundle that contained our weapons, among them two harquebuses, which Lucía, Rubén, and I unwrapped and loaded. We also loaded the falconet on the port side with cannonballs. Then my godfather turned it to aim at the poop deck.

"Have the fuse ready and look alive," he ordered.

Rubén the black sat down beneath the falconet. Lucía and I took over one harquebus and my godfather the other, propping them on the railing.

CHAPTER VII

The crewmen kicked and pounded on the captain's door in a fury. Then they ran up the ladders and, after a long hard struggle, tore the weather-deck falconet, which was attached to the gunwale, from its forked prop, and hauled it to the poop deck. They tied it on some beams with rope, a few steps from the captain's cabin, its mouth aimed at the door. The sailors searched the bundles of cargo for a barrel of gunpowder and for cannonballs.

In the midst of this mayhem, my godfather began waving his arms. "I swear to Juan Lamas," he thundered, "I've put up with enough of your madness! In the name of the Crown of Thorns, have done with this now! Stop, in the name of all the devils!"

The men stopped what they were doing, and stood

there looking at my godfather as though seeing him for the first time. They saw our harquebuses and saw Rubén, with his arm around the falconet on our end of the deck, pointing it straight at them and holding the lighted fuse in his other hand.

An elderly sailor stepped forward, to the edge of the forecastle deck. "We're hungry," he called out.

"I know," my godfather replied. "We will share with you our scant stores of water and food, and, if necessary, we will sacrifice our mounts to feed everyone. But you must put an end to this rioting and hand over the gunpowder and cannonballs to me."

The crew formed a tight circle and spoke among themselves. Frequently, a wrathful exclamation, or a swearword, punctuated their heated discussion. When they were done, one of the older sailors, the steward, assumed the role of spokesman for the group. He crossed over to our side of the pool of water on the deck and spoke in measured tones.

"Sir," he addressed my godfather. "We gratefully accept Your Grace's offer. But, if necessary, we will also use our captain's mascot for food, since the Almighty created the animals of the world in the hierarchical order, to ensure the survival of the children of Eve."

"The matter will be settled when the proper time comes," my godfather replied.

To reach our side, the sailors rigged up a sort of platform using a couple of empty barrels, on which they placed the kegs of gunpowder and the sack of cannonballs. The pool of water that covered the deck was truly an extraordinary sight: floating in it were drowned rats, mismatched shoes, empty bottles, and other objects from the flooded hold.

Solemnly, my godfather divided the food into as many shares as there were members of the ship's company, including a share for the captain and another for the boatswain, and filled a small leather flask with a similar number of measures of fresh water.

"At this same hour tomorrow, I will give you another day's rations," he said.

Four more days went by, and the food as well as the water were almost gone. The fodder for our mounts was also running out, despite the fact that we had given them scant rations and they had scarcely tasted the water.

"We are going to have to do away with those animals," Godfather said. "Too bad that we didn't save some of the sacks of salt so as to cure their meat."

Later on, he seemed less resolute. "Why sacrifice them?" he said. "Our fate is decided. The right thing to do is make our peace with the Lord and prepare to die with dignity."

The meager rations made us all weak and drowsy. As for the ship, it followed the course set by the wind, which blew in whatever direction it pleased.

One morning, the sun already high in the sky, I was awakened by a strange tapping sound. Except for the tapping and the creaking plaints of the rigging, silence reigned throughout the ship, and my comrades in the forecastle as well as the sailors on the poop deck were sleeping as motionless as corpses. I noted with concern that the water was now so high that the gunwale was no longer visible above the surface.

The tapping sound continued and as I looked around I saw its source: a dark-colored bird was pecking in the dung of our mounts. I bounded to my feet and the bird flew off. I gazed into the distance and discerned the faint outline of the coast.

"Land!" I shouted. "Land-ho!" And I shouted until everyone was awake. Even the captain, who came running out of his cabin, climbed to the poop deck and avidly scrutinized the horizon. He finally said something that, though we didn't hear his exact words, was met with shouts of joy from the crew.

"Captain, are you familiar with this island?" my godfather asked.

"It's not an island," said the captain. "Judging from its shape and orientation, I would swear that we are off Yucatan, between Campeche and Champotón. They call that shape that protrudes the Devil's Snout."

That day no one felt hungry or thirsty. We all leaned on the gunwale, watching the coast get closer and more distinct. When night fell, we spied a dim light on shore—to us, a sure sign of human habitation, of food and rest.

We scarcely slept. The ship made very little headway, but neither the strength of the wind nor its direction changed. It was dawn before we could clearly distinguish higher ground, farther in the distance, and the dense line of trees that marked the shoreline.

The boat drifted for yet another day, as we gazed helplessly at the unreachable shore. Finally, we caught a current that brought us closer, and before long we found ourselves sailing toward a wide beach. The wind was in our favor and at last the ship ran aground, dragging on the bottom for a long time with a noise resembling a deep grunt. It was a good time to run aground; it was low tide and a big stretch of beach lay before us. Unloading the mounts was hard, but we managed to get them to swim to shore, and all three reached land safe and sound. Empty casks served as lifebuoys and floats for our bundles. Soon we were all on the beach.

But before we disembarked, something happened that left us distressed. As the sailors were getting some boats ready, the captain's mascot emerged from the cabin and in a flash leaped over the gunwale and plunged into the sea. The captain shouted to it at the top of his lungs, but the animal's white body drew farther and farther away, swimming swiftly. Then the boatswain, after removing his blouse and his breeches, also dove into the sea, and we watched him swim after the creature for a long time, paying no heed to our shouts until, no doubt exhausted, he disappeared beneath the waters.

Expending our last stores of energy, we loaded our worn-out mules and sought shelter under the trees. By noon, we had set up camp next to a small freshwater stream. The men gathered a great deal of fruit, which we ate until we were sated, as though it were the most delicious of viands. And then we rested in the shade of the wood, all of us indifferent to any danger that might lie before us.

CHAPTER VIII

We camped there for several days, recovering our strength. Our fruit diet was eventually supplemented with fish, shellfish, and even two deer that Godfather and Rubén bagged. The mounts grazed amid the trees, and the warm weather made our rest all the more pleasant.

A high tide brought in the boatswain's body, which we buried at the edge of the beach. The high tides were also bringing the caravel closer to shore.

With the loss of the boatswain and his mascot, the captain had plunged into a profound depression, from which he finally emerged like someone who realizes that he has been living in a dream. I was near him when it happened. It was shortly after noon one day and we were all resting among the trees, sheltered from the scorching sun, which was hidden only in midmorning and late-afternoon downpours.

All of a sudden, the captain leaped to his feet and shouted: "It wasn't a siren. Didn't you see it? It was only a bewitchment, a spell."

He ran toward the beach, where he cursed and shouted for some time. Finally he came back, dripping with sweat, then collapsed on the ground and remained there, motionless, all day long, gazing out to sea with a sickly expression on his face.

Dawn the following day found him in the same position but somehow his mood had been transformed. He gave the order for assembly and instructed his men that as much as possible be recovered from the ship, to help us in constructing a brigantine that would get us away from these shores.

The ship was now so close that at low tide the sailors could reach it in shallow water. They began to salvage implements and equipment, stripping the ship of everything that might prove useful.

The captain insisted that we were on the west coast of Yucatan. We were told that the building of the brigantine and its preparation for setting sail would delay our departure for the greater part of two months; and, the vessel would be a very crude one. With such a craft, and being obliged to sail with the prevailing north winds—which, according to the sailors, were characteristic of the season and would soon begin to rise—we would have to follow the coastline, making our voyage even longer and more arduous, whether we chose to head for Nombre de Dios or to return to our point of departure, the port of Veracruz. Forced to wait, my godfather was in quite a bad humor.

"We would have done better to confront the dangers of the overland route, Miguel," my godfather said. "In my experience, sea journeys always are ill-fated."

However, one day we had news. We were hauling trees that had just been felled to the area designated as the shipyard, when a loud voice ordered us to halt in His Majesty's name. In seconds, a company of soldiers had surrounded us. Though the barrels of their harquebuses and the blades of their halberds glinted in the sun, their ragged and tattered uniforms showed that they must have been far from their headquarters for some time.

A man wearing a burnished helmet, mounted on a good-looking horse, stood out from the foot soldiers. "Who's in command here?" he asked. "Where are you people from?"

"We were shipwrecked, sir," our captain replied. "I am the captain—despite the fact that the ship has now been taken apart."

The man in the helmet dismounted and withdrew with the ship's captain to a patch of shade. He interrogated him as to our place of origin and our destination, maintaining an attitude of reserve and even of suspicion, until he had a full and minutely detailed explanation of the circumstances surrounding our shipwreck.

The troops belonged to the army of don Francisco de Montejo, the son of the Adelantado of the same name to whom the Emperor had granted the right to command an expedition to discover and conquer Yucatan. On catching sight of us, they had been afraid that we, too, were an expedition of discoverers and they were prepared to defend, to the point of violence, their exclusive right of conquest.

We found out that don Francisco de Montejo's army was scattered throughout a vast expanse of territory, and had fought a great battle with the native Indians, whom they had defeated.

My godfather's credentials finally calmed the anxieties of their commander, for they proved to him my godfather's status as a discoverer of islands and a conquistador of Mexico, a subject that led to lively conversation.

One of the cavalrymen accompanying the troops of soldiers took great interest in my godfather's story. He was a man with ashen skin, straight black hair, and a sparse black beard. He was dressed in dark-colored garments which did not seem to be as tattered and badly worn as those of the rest of the men.

He was a bachelor-at-arms, the counselor of the Adelantado himself, who was accompanying the patrol to verify the limits of the pacification as well as the situation in the conquered territories. He had two servants, one of them a mulatto and the other a Spaniard, who was deaf.

The bachelor and my godfather were engaged in a friendly chat for some time. The bachelor handled my godfather's credentials as though they were sacred objects.

"You are truly fortunate," he commented. "Not only because of the great honor attached to your mission, but because you will be carrying it out in the provinces of Peru, of which so many marvels have been recounted. It is clear that you have good friends there."

"It is a great honor for my humble person, but I do not owe it to friends. It was a chance meeting with one of His Majesty's inspectors, whom I have not seen again, for he is still in Spain, that was the source of the post assigned me. Bear in mind that my friends stayed behind in Mexico or Guatemala, if they did not meet their deaths. I know no one in the territory of Peru. Not even the chief magistrate of the Royal Tribunal of Panama, in whose service I am about to be engaged."

My godfather broke off for a moment, as though hesitating, and then went on. "They say that the battles between the partisans of Almagro and Pizarro have reduced those lands to wrack and ruin."

The bachelor handed my godfather the envelope with his credentials. "But the war will end and the land and the mines and the Indians will still be there. After so much armed combat, you may be sure that this is a moment that truly favors your destiny."

My godfather nodded, as though silently in agreement with the words that the other man had spoken; but then he gave a sigh.

"Aren't you content?" the bachelor asked.

"It's not possible for me to be content," my godfather replied. "We have lost the ship that was transporting us, and in the building of a crude imitation of a ship we will lose many more days. The Almighty alone knows when we will reach Panama, and after that, the port of El Callao. That is what spoils my pleasure at the prospect of things to come."

After a pause, the bachelor spoke slowly. He had a persuasive tone that reminded me of men of the cloth.

"My dear friend," he said, "I would advise you not to wait for this vessel to be set afloat. As you know, the days of the prevailing wind from the north are close at hand, and whatever course you follow, the voyage is going to be very slow and arduous."

"What can I do, then?" my godfather exclaimed.

"You have mounts. Heading east across the peninsula will take you back to a coast that is well traveled, with the possibility of finding a ship returning to Nombre de Dios, the same ship that brings our army's rations. You would have to cover sixty leagues at most."

"But we are not familiar with the area."

"This area is almost completely pacified and to the east there is no resistance at all. I can accompany you for several days' journey. After that, you will be certain to find guides."

I could see that my godfather's spirits were reviving. "When do you leave?"

"Tomorrow at first light," the bachelor-at-arms replied. "I must return first to my lord don Francisco, who at present is north of here, seeking the best place to found a city to commemorate his victory. I must then continue eastward, to check on how the conquest is going."

They went on talking together, absorbed in their conversation.

Lucía approached and discreetly gestured me away from them.

"What is it?" I asked her.

"I called you aside because of what that man's servants have been up to," she answered in a low voice. "I found them going through our equipment."

"Going through it?"

"Taking out various things, the weapons, the clothes. I asked what they were doing and they were startled. Then one said that it was all an unfortunate error. Doesn't that strike you as peculiar?"

I shrugged.

"Miguel, I don't like these people."

"Well, they're going to be our traveling companions," I said. "Don Santiago isn't going to wait for the ship to be finished. He wants us to proceed overland."

"Tell him that I found the men rummaging in our things."

When the bachelor-at-arms and my godfather bade each other goodbye, I told my godfather, but he gave no importance whatever to the incident. His mind was wholly on our departure.

"We leave at dawn," he said. "We must load a mule with as much as it can carry. You and I will ride on horseback, so as not to lessen our dignity in the eyes of the bachelor-at-arms. Lucía can share your mount. As for the business about the servants, I'll complain about it, so that they'll be reprimanded."

CHAPTER IX

Our little expeditionary force left the next morning as the crewmen were beginning to toil yet another day at building the brigantine. The bachelor-at-arms, who was on horseback, was accompanied by two servants, each on a mule, and five foot soldiers, one of them carrying an harquebus. My godfather was riding his horse and Lucía and I were astride a mule, with one of our bundles. The rest of our supplies were carried on the back of our third mount, which Rubén led by its halter. Behind our group followed a silent party of Indians, a number of whom were shackled like slaves. They carried the goods of the bachelor-at-arms and his company of foot soldiers.

We soon reached a broad plain with groves of different kinds of trees. It was extremely hot, but the shade of the thick foliage provided some relief. The wood resounded with the flapping of wings and the songs of many birds.

We were all silent, save for the bachelor-at-arms and my godfather. The bachelor repeatedly marveled at my godfather's promising future.

Lucía, who held fast to my waist with both arms, gave me a squeeze each time she heard one of his flattering remarks. "I don't like that man," she whispered in my ear, in the old language.

I shrugged. I had no set opinion about the bachelor-at-arms—he seemed friendly enough.

The conversation between my godfather and the bachelor turned again and again to the benefices and profits of various posts and offices. I was surprised that my godfather, a man who had never given any signs of worldly ambition, had undergone such a change. The bachelor-at-arms confessed his aspiration to be named *corregidor,* municipal magistrate, when the Adelantado whom he served had founded his city.

"A post as city magistrate by royal decree," he said. "Since he does not have enough Indian laborers to grant to those who deserve them under the encomienda system."

"And is that territory very rich?" my godfather asked.

"The Indians call it the land of turkey and deer, and in all truth there is such a variety of game it's a miracle. Sisal, maize, cotton, cocoa beans, and many different fruits are also produced in abundance. And there is a great deal of salt, to the north."

"And what about gold?"

The bachelor-at-arms made a gesture of annoyance.

"That is the one thing that is lacking for these regions to be another Mexico, another Peru. There is no gold, or precious stones, or pearls."

In the course of the day's journey we saw some of the results of the war: the remains of a settlement that had been burned to the ground, and maize fields where grain, which should be ready for harvesting, had been abandoned, without any sign of cultivation. On the second day's journey, the consequences of war were more macabre still: we came across more towns destroyed by recent fires, and under a pandemonium of birds of prey, a tree with its branches laden with the bodies of hanged Indian warriors. At the foot of the tree lay scattered and broken weapons—heavy wooden clubs, bows and arrows, and lances—that the Indians had brandished when alive.

There was an unbearable stench of rotting flesh in the air. We stopped up our nostrils and quickened our pace to get past the spot as soon as possible.

"My lord," my godfather said to the bachelor-at-arms, "it is one of the works of charity to bury the dead."

"They have doubtless been left there to serve as an example and a warning," the bachelor commented. "The peoples of this region have endured great suffering as a result of our conquest, but their resistance had to be broken by a great force of arms and there was much bloodshed on the part of our troops. Captain don Justino de Corcos is in charge of pacifying these territories, and he is severe when it comes to any rebellion."

The sight of the tree was awesome, and many of the Indians in our escort party wept aloud, lamenting in their own language. I did not understand them, but Lucía recognized some familiar words. She squeezed my waist again.

"What is it?" I asked.

"I understand them!" she whispered to me. "Their language is similar to the one my people spoke."

"What are they saying?"

"They are grieving for everything that they've lost."

A vast wood then separated us from the scenes of devastation and death. But on the third day we emerged from the forest into another area of cultivation that had been abandoned, with the remains of dwellings that had been burned to the ground. The few people we saw took to their heels in terror as we passed. In the distance an incessant flapping of wings over one of the trees reminded us of the macabre sights of the day before. As we got closer, we were able to make out another execution tree, its branches laden with human figures.

"Let's get out of here," my godfather said.

But something about the tree had attracted his attention, for suddenly his gaze shifted, and drawing away from us, he put the spurs to his horse and rode toward it. He halted at the foot of the tree stared at it intently, as our expeditionary force proceeded apace. Finally, my godfather turned his mount around, and I stopped to wait for him. He was crestfallen and his face was pale.

"What's the matter, Godfather?" I asked.

"Come, Miguel," he said with a sigh. "Let's get away from here."

When we caught up with the rest of the party, my godfather sought out the bachelor-at-arms. Once at his side, my godfather burst out in a loud, indignant voice.

"Sir," he said, "I have just witnessed an example of the kind of pacification that your army is carrying out in these lands, and I assure you that I plan to take my protest to His Majesty and demand rightful punishment for such cruelty."

The bachelor-at-arms looked at my godfather bewildered.

"Bachelor, in that execution tree there were no male warriors, but women, and children hanging from their mothers' feet," he said.

The bachelor-at-arms gave a start.

"Are those the orders of your Adelantado?" asked my godfather.

"No," replied the bachelor. "Under no circumstances must such a thought enter your mind. Don Francisco de Montejo the younger is a man as liberal and generous as his father and utterly opposed to any sort of cruelty. Bear in mind that at present there is little control of the regular army troops, as they are widely scattered."

"But yesterday you told me that there is someone in command of the soldiers in this region."

"Captain Justino de Corcos. We're heading for his camp."

"Well, then I will demand of him a full explanation of these atrocities."

The bachelor-at-arms said nothing, and an uninterrupted silence replaced the animated conversation in which the two of them had engaged during the last few days.

It must have been midmorning on the following day when we arrived at the camp of Captain Justino de

Corcos. The camp was situated on a spacious plain, where maize must have been liberally sowed earlier on, judging from the dried-up stalks, and where many sisal plants thrived. The camp was surrounded by a wooden palisade.

Entering the camp took a good while, since the corps of camp guards, after the bachelor-at-arms introduced us, required that we produce detailed identification. The Indian porters—called *tamemes* in my part of the country—were sent off to an area outside the camp.

The slow process of getting into the camp, which obliged us to stand in the sun, and how little his credentials seemed to impress the officer in charge of the guards, put my godfather in a bad mood. Once we had been allowed inside, he asked to see the captain, who agreed to receive him when the heat of the day began to subside. The bachelor-at-arms and I accompanied him.

Captain Justino de Corcos was a thin man, with faded chestnut-colored hair and beard. He had a solemn, even surly, face. When he spoke, the surliness took on a harsher tone because he was missing an eyetooth and several other teeth in his upper jaw, the result no doubt of a violent fight.

The captain was standing in the middle of the large circular tent which served him both as living quarters and as headquarters. He was going over a document that he had dictated to his scribe, and it was some time before he turned his attention to us.

My godfather introduced himself, mentioning his status as one of the conquistadors of Mexico, and his new post. Then, without further preamble, he asked, in a haughty voice, for an explanation of the execution of the innocents whom he had seen hanging from the tree.

The captain grasped the hilt of his sword. "My dear sir," he said coldly, "we recently won a great victory, after a fierce battle, and now we are consolidating our rule. I shall put down any rebellion even if I am forced to kill off all the Indians in this territory, be they young lads or old men, damsels or suckling babes."

"But you must know that His Majesty has repeatedly ordered that the natives be treated well; that they not suffer harm or mistreatment; and that any harm done them be punished."

The captain let out a burst of hollow laughter.

"Why all that laughter?" demanded my godfather. He, too, had grasped the hilt of his sword and his face was flushed with anger.

"You just said that you had taken part in the conquest of Mexico," replied the captain. "Have you forgotten the military expedition against Cholula? It is said that you took hundreds of natives by surprise, and killed every last one of them."

My godfather snorted. "We had to forestall a plot against us, Captain. But in no instance were we the murderers of mothers and defenseless children. I shall see to it that the proper weight is accorded my testimony concerning the savagery of your troops, for which I hold you responsible. I assure you that just as God looks down upon us with his infinite eye, so will I make you pay for your excesses."

The captain replied in a loud and sullen voice. "I have fought for ten years to conquer this land of Yucatan. I have had many an exhausting day and bear many a scar. On one occasion I was forced to abandon the mission, leaving behind a good number of dead comrades. I, too, have paid a price in my own blood. Take your complaint to whomever you please. But I have no obligation to extend my hospitality to you and your company. I shall not oblige you to leave the camp at this instant, because at this hour it would jeopardize everyone's safety to alter the guards' routine. But tomorrow morning, after reveille, you must leave. And tonight you will be under the surveillance of my men."

Soldiers surrounded us. My godfather unsheathed his sword in wrath, struck the pommel with his hand, then turned around and left the tent. I followed him, but I could see that the bachelor-at-arms stayed behind, conversing with the captain in a low and hurried voice.

We would take shelter for the night in a shed made of dry branches, similar to a small Indian hut. It was almost dark, but I could see a soldier standing guard at the entrance to our rough shed and two others patrolling outside, pacing slowly back and forth along the four walls. My godfather looked in fury at the soldier by the door, who quickly approached, calling us excitedly by name: "Don Santiago, Miguel."

I recognized him immediately. It was Juan García, the Sevillian, a survivor like us of the disastrous expedition to find and conquer the kingdom of Yupaha, whom we had last seen when, in the company of a man from Trujillo, he was about to depart for Veracruz, to return to Spain and improve the prospects of the family business, thanks to the riches he had come by.

"Let's not talk now," he said quickly. "When my watch is over, I will come and speak with you."

I waited impatiently. When it had grown pitch-dark, we heard the guard changing. Then someone muttered a few words and came into the shed, carrying a small hooded lantern that, when uncovered, gave a faint light. It was the Sevillian.

He told us that he had not been able to return to Spain. He and his comrade, once they reached the Villa Rica de la Vera Cruz, had got caught up in a long game of cards that ate up every bit of money the two of them had earned. They had signed on as sailors on one of the boats heading for Panama, but he had jumped ship in Cozumel when he heard about the new campaign to conquer Yucatan led by the son of don Francisco de Montejo. He had enlisted and had taken part in the great final battle and now in the work of pacification.

"You can't be very proud of the tasks assigned you," my godfather said. "I have seen how you hanged children from the dead bodies of their mothers."

Juan García hesitated a few seconds. "It's the captain, my lord don Santiago. The captain and three of his lieutenants are indescribably cruel. Even with Christians. I have seen savage punishments meted out to soldiers in this camp. I myself am perhaps risking my life at this moment by coming here."

"Didn't the sentry see you?"

"He saw me. But I told him that you were friends of mine, and he, too, has had his fill of such stern discipline and so many atrocities."

He then told us that the captain, in order to put an end

to the insubordination of the conquered Indians, inflicted terrible reprisals on the villages that gave shelter or food to the few surviving insurgents.

"At times his cruelty seems to us to be the devil's doing. At this very moment he is holding as prisoners in this camp, with the intention of hanging them, two Indian girls, twin sisters, whose sole crime is the fact that they are beautiful. Most of the soldiers pity them, which the captain claims is proof that the two damsels have upset the entire camp. By killing them, he says, he will show the Indians that Spaniards are not moved to pity by women, however pretty."

Juan García sighed. My godfather gave him a pat on the back. He covered the lantern again and went off, and we lay there, wide awake, not saying a word, for a long time.

CHAPTER X

When reveille sounded, we were already preparing to leave, and had been for some time. After what we had heard about the unrest in the territory, we took all precautions. I dressed in one of the cotton hauberks that my mother and Micaela had made for me, and on top of it I slung several belts on which to hang my crossbow and my quiver loaded with arrows. My brand-new sword was at my side.

As we passed one of the huts in the camp, we could see, by the light of early dawn, two feminine figures, no doubt the young Indian girls. They were wearing white *huipiles*, and their hands were bound in stocks, chained to a post. They were very beautiful, and in their lovely features and dark eyes, identical in their two faces, was an expression of great sadness.

We were going through the main gate when the bachelor-at-arms and his retinue approached. Outside, prepared to follow, were the group of Indian porters. The bachelor-at-arms came over to my godfather, who gazed at him with a stern, cold look on his face.

"Your Excellency don Santiago," the bachelor-at-arms said, "I didn't want you to march off alone, since I share your indignation. If you will permit me, I wish to add my testimony to yours to denounce the villainies of this tyrannical captain."

My godfather's frown disappeared. "I bid you welcome, sir, and forgive me if your close ties to the Adelantado of these troops of militia aroused in me certain reservations about you. But your attitude is clear proof that one can tell a sheep from a goat."

Just then a cavalryman rode up to the portcullis at full gallop and pressed the guards to let him in immediately.

"Indians," he said, on being questioned by the bachelor-at-arms. "A great number of Indian rebels are gathering south of here."

As we proceeded on our way, we could hear the sounds and the shouts of preparations being made in the camp.

"Let us make haste," the bachelor-at-arms said. "We are heading north, where it is not likely that we will encounter any danger."

We went on in silence for several hours. It seemed the prediction of the bachelor-at-arms was coming true, for we did not come across any Indian warriors. We proceeded through the jungle, and occasionally, through gaps in the masses of foliage, we caught glimpses of worked stone—made by human hands—abandoned long before and now covered with tangled vegetation.

In answer to my godfather's questions, the bachelor-at-arms explained that buildings of great beauty—with detailed carvings, some of which were painted in marvelous colors—were scattered throughout Yucatan. It was a mystery how those buildings had been constructed without metal tools by a people who, judging from the sculpted figures, were ancestors of today's Indians, though they seemed to have had far more robust bodies than their descendants.

He also said that, to all appearances, the ancient Indians had known great prosperity, though it was at a time when, for unknown reasons, they were wont to relocate their settlements periodically, building new cities and abandoning the ones in which they had lived before.

We camped at the foot of a gigantic ceiba tree. My godfather was all ears as he listened to the stories of the bachelor-at-arms. The latter told him that there was one of those ancient abandoned cities near the route we were following. It had buildings whose size and beautiful workmanship were amazing, huge temples, vast theaters, and a giant pit more than a hundred feet wide with a drop of fifteen *estados*—about a hundred feet down to the water level—where the ancient Indians offered human beings in abominable sacrifices. Apparently, they also threw many treasures into the pit, meant to lie there submerged for all time.

The description of the marvels of this city and the secrets of the great pit aroused my godfather's lively curiosity. "Wouldn't it be possible for us to see the city?" he asked.

The question filled the bachelor-at-arms with satisfaction.

"Certainly," he said. "But despite the fact that it is close to our route and that the city itself has excellent roads, it is cut off from our route by dense vegetation, which may cause difficulties for our foot soldiers and *tamemes*."

My godfather looked a little regretful; and finally the bachelor-at-arms suggested that perhaps the foot soldiers could go on following the set route—keeping an eye on the slaves and the *tamemes*—while those of us with mounts might detour to the city, since for us the trip would be quick and easy.

And so we accepted his proposal, though Lucía preferred to stay with Rubén, the better to look after our equipment and provisions. The next morning, as the foot soldiers and the bearers went on their way, the bachelor-at-arms, along with his two servants, my godfather, and I set out for the city. As a precaution, I took with me two extra quivers of arrows. As for my godfather, he put all our gold in the leather pouch with his credentials and hung it around his neck, under his hauberk.

The jungle was full of gentle sounds. The birds, the monkeys, the butterflies, sudden movements among the branches, reminded us that the jungle was teeming with life. At times I thought we were lost, but after about three hours of traveling, we arrived at a wide, white roadway which, despite the overgrown vegetation, was still visible on the floor of the jungle.

"Roads like these joined one settlement to another," the bachelor-at-arms explained. "Today almost all of them have been devoured by the jungle. This is one of the entrances to the city."

We followed the road and soon came to a place where the jungle gave way to enormous geometrical buildings. Although trees and underbrush had taken root in the areas that had once been avenues and public squares, and the buildings, too, were overgrown with vegetation, we could see that without a doubt it had been an immense and very beautiful city. Visible through the dense vegetation, the buildings were silent and appeared to be deserted, like gigantic corpses that still had a melancholy look about them. The sounds of the jungle seemed fainter here, as though in respect for the emptiness once occupied by human beings.

Each building was different from the others. One was on top of a large platform; it was very broad but not very high, and it had a long façade supported by pillars. The façade had many doors. The huge size of the building and its harmonious proportions impressed my godfather, who swore that he had never seen anything like it, except in the ancient capital of Mexico. There were also enormous pyramidal buildings, one of them very high, with rounded sides, flanked by two dizzying staircases.

The quality and homogeneity of the stonework complemented the rich adornment of the whole. Bas-reliefs, executed with meticulous attention to detail, followed complicated patterns over the walls of all the buildings.

"This must have been a most civilized city, surely. Its inhabitants were builders of genius," my godfather remarked.

Near the area that the bachelor-at-arms called a theater—an open space between two huge platforms—our attention was attracted by a pile of rounded stones resembling corpses: an ominous symbol of all the mute devastation.

After wandering up and down the ancient streets, we halted at the foot of a pyramid where a group of monkeys were making a commotion.

"And what about the famous pit?" my godfather asked.

"Follow me," the bachelor-at-arms said. "We must take that road."

We left the buildings behind us, taking a broad white path that led to a clearing. Except for a small stone hut, there were no other buildings to be seen.

We dismounted and went on for a few yards, toward the stone hut. All of a sudden we were able to see, just beyond the hut, a huge opening in the ground. The sun clearly marked the steep drop-off, a wall of bare stone that came to an end far below, a distance of more than twenty meters. The water at the bottom was of such vastness that a caravel could sail on it. The water glimmered with a green light, giving off a reflection at once vegetable and mineral, of luxuriant plants and precious stone.

My godfather and I approached the very edge and gazed in amazement at the extraordinary lake. But we had another reason to be amazed. For the voice of the bachelor-at-arms rang out behind us, without its usual courteous, and even servile, modulations now, ordering us to be silent. We turned and saw his servants aiming a crossbow at each of us. Their attitude was resolute and cruel.

"Keep still," the bachelor-at-arms ordered. "Your lives depend on it."

He was holding his sword with the point directed at my godfather's breast. "Hand over your leather pouch, don Santiago."

My godfather had been rendered mute from this turn of events.

I seized the hilt of my sword and the deaf servant came out with a growl that seemed more like a wild beast's.

"Unsheathe one handsbreadth of that sword and my faithful Pascualillo will send two handspans of a crossbow arrow into your gut, my lad," the bachelor-at-arms said through clenched teeth.

"Stay still, Miguel, my boy," my godfather said, having finally recovered his powers of speech. "Rabid dogs don't growl for no reason."

He took out the small leather pouch in which he carried his credentials and our gold, pulling the thong over his head.

"You really fooled us," he said bitterly.

He threw the leather pouch on the ground, at the feet of the bachelor-at-arms, who cautiously crouched down to pick it up, never taking his eyes off my godfather. Once he had the pouch in his hands, he stepped back, undid the thongs, and quickly examined the contents.

"Everything is in good order, my lord don Santiago,"

he said, grinning. "Rest assured that I will know how to honor these titles and this wealth."

He cast a glance at the servants, who, with the breech of their crossbows resting between shoulder and armpit, were aiming at us most carefully. I saw the point of the arrow directed at my throat and Pascualillo's right eye filled with an evil gleam, and realized they were going to do us in at that very moment.

"Jump, Miguel," my godfather called out.

I flung myself into the abyss, feeling the arrow's whistle just over my head. I experienced the long fall as an endless, breathless pause. At long last, my body hit the water. At that depth, there was a coolness that testified to the fact that the jungle, even though so near, was in a different realm.

My godfather fell in just after I did. I heard a great splash as his body hit the water, reverberating in a dull echo. Then, suddenly aware of the great silence, I saw my godfather floating face down. I swam toward him, and as I took hold of his body, my hand grazed against the shaft of an arrow. I was heartsick when I realized that the arrow had hit him right on target, but I did my best to keep myself and my godfather afloat as I looked for a handhold.

CHAPTER XI

"Godfather! Godfather!" I shouted. He opened his eyes. I was clinging precariously to a rough stone outcropping in the wall.

"Miguel, my boy," he said. "It seems that they got me."

A short distance away, I caught sight of some roots at water level that might serve as a better handhold. "Come on, Godfather, try."

We slowly made our way over and managed to grab hold of them. I tried to take a look at his wound, but he was wearing his coat of mail, in case of a skirmish with the Indians; it was not easy to examine the extent and depth of the wound caused by an arrow that had been able to pierce the coat of mail.

To spare ourselves unnecessary effort, I knew we both had to rid ourselves of our garments and our weapons. I let my sword and my crossbow sink to the bottom of the lake and used my baldrics to tie my godfather to the thick roots that grew out of the rocky wall. After I took off my boots and my cotton hauberk, it was much easier for me to move about.

Removing my godfather's garments was a slow, difficult process. First, I had to extract the arrow, trying my best not to leave a single fragment embedded. I made every effort not to hurt him, but he sighed and moaned sharply, in obvious pain.

"Godfather," I said to him, "I have to pull it out."

Because the weapon had been fired at him from close range, the coat of mail had not prevented the arrow from piercing his body, but his armor had deflected its aim. My godfather must have moved at the moment the arrow was released, for it had lodged sideways in his shoulder. I braced my feet on the wall, took hold of the arrow with my right hand, as close as possible to the wound, and pulled. My godfather gave a great moan, but the arrow came out all in one piece.

I then divested him of his sword and also removed his boots, his doublet, and the coat of mail. The wound bled profusely and with strips torn from one of my sleeves I bandaged it as best I could. Then I pulled the baldrics even tighter around my godfather's body till he was securely tied to the roots. Only his head showed above the water. His eyes were closed and he looked in bad shape.

After all this, I gripped the roots with one hand, and tried to rest for a while. I knew we were in grave danger and that it was my responsibility not to let pass a chance to get out of it, if such a chance existed.

By temperament I am more inclined toward dreaming than toward action, but the adventures in which I had participated a year before had taught me, among other things, that no temperament inevitably determines the ability to act in the most expedient way when necessary. And even though I tend to feel emotions strongly, I firmly resolved to keep a cool head and keep on the alert, so that my spirits wouldn't fall into a dejection that might bring our end sooner, if such was the aim of fickle fortune.

Seen from the surface of the water, the wall of bare stone was even more awesome, because of its height and inaccessibility, than when viewed from ground level. I explored a long section of it, in search of a way to climb out, but by nightfall I still had not found anything, and so I returned to my godfather's side.

Our view of the night sky was limited by the dimensions of the mouth of the pit; around it, there was total darkness. It was a moonless night, but there were no clouds, and the circle enclosed within those enormous walls sparkled with bright stars, whose radiance was reflected in the mirror of the still waters.

Several exotic birds at the top of the cliff began to sing their melancholy song seemingly in time to the pulsation of the stars—a sound appropriate to our predicament, adding to the sensation that we had left life and the earth behind and were at the portals of a nocturnal, subterranean world, where the only thing left was to accept oblivion and death with resignation.

It then seemed to me that I intuited something of the terrible meaning of the ritual sacrifices that, according to the traitorous bachelor-at-arms, took place in these waters, when boys and girls were thrown in to be drowned. I also discerned a strange meaning to the fact that gold and precious objects lay submerged there. A gentle sense of despair threatened to take possession of my will, and I was forced to make extraordinary efforts to keep up my spirits.

The next day, the sun beat down on us. My godfather was badly hurt, but clearheaded. I told him that I was going to go around the entire perimeter of the great pit, to re-examine the walls, minutely, and went off. I was quite weak and was obliged to proceed slowly.

Shortly before midday, I was halfway around—exactly across from where my godfather was—and I had not found any ledges or stepping-stones that might serve as a way out. But as the sun lit up the opposite side of the pit, I saw something that gave my heart a start: in the wall of the steep cliff, directly above my godfather, was the shadow of what looked like a large cave.

I went back to my godfather filled with hope, but took care not to exhaust myself. After so many hours in the water, my limbs had grown numb and my muscles ached.

When I reached my godfather's side, I clambered up the roots and began to search for a way up the cliffside. Knowing that the hollow space above us might be our only chance for survival, I felt my agility and my strength increase. My fingers grasped the least tiny concave space, and my feet found a hold in the slightest roughness of the rock. Finally, as I felt about with my hands, I made out the angle of a ledge and, after a great deal of effort, managed to pull myself up into the cave.

It was a huge hollow space, no doubt made by landslides of long ago. Perhaps water had once flowed through it. To the left of the entrance I noticed a big bundle of thick, interwoven roots. The cave was as high as two men and about as wide, and appeared to be quite long, for despite the brightness of the sun—which turned the entire surface of the water a gleaming green—the back of the cave was invisible in the semidarkness.

I entered the shadowed area and reached the darkest part, then went on in complete darkness, at an angle sloping upward. Though imperceptible at first, I felt a growing current of air. I supposed that that narrow subterranean gallery must lead to another, larger space, so I went back to the entrance, forcing myself not to give a shout proclaiming my discovery.

I dived into the water, above which countless butterflies fluttered, and swam to my godfather. He opened his eyes and looked at me. He was very pale.

"Godfather," I said, as firmly as I could, "there's a cave in the side of the cliff. I think it's a way out of here. We must climb up to it. We may be able to survive this."

He looked at me quietly. "I don't know if I can move, Miguel. I shall try. But listen: if I am unable to get out, you must go. You are not to stay here. Swear to me, this very minute, or else I won't even try."

"Come on, Godfather, be still. Save your breath."

"Swear, Miguel."

"I promise, don Santiago."

He looked at me with implacable calm.

"I swear," I added. "Yes, I swear, but let's go now, and God help us."

We began then, making extended and painful efforts. My godfather seemed to be paralyzed after being in the water motionless for so long, and his wound, which had never ceased causing him pain, must have been unbearable as he tried to move. He fought hard, and both of us struggled to lift his body over the roots, but without success.

It occurred to me that perhaps the baldrics that had held him above the water for so long might be of use. I climbed up to the mouth of the cave and tied the end of a baldric to one of the roots just inside the entrance. I let the strap dangle down and held on to it, my body serving as a ladder for my godfather, who groped his way up until his feet rested on the top of the roots that protruded above the water. He was so weak that tears brimmed over from his eyes like the trickle of a little stream.

When he reached as far up as I was, I tied the baldric to his good arm, clambered up to the cave once again, all out of breath now, and began to hoist him up, using the roots as capstans. My pulling and his impassioned determination to get out, his helping himself as best he could with his legs and with his good arm grasping the rough outcroppings of the wall, finally met with success. He collapsed at the mouth of the cave, where we both lay stretched out, exhausted.

Darkness fell and I dropped off to sleep. When I woke up, the sun was high in the sky, and I found myself dry and in fine spirits, though very hungry. My godfather, however, was feverish. His wound, which had stopped bleeding, looked purulent and the flesh around the edges was badly inflamed.

"Godfather," I said, "I'm going to see where the cave leads."

I don't know if he heard me. He muttered unintelligibly and was motionless, collapsed on the ground. I went off into the darkness.

It was the slight air current that encouraged me to go on, for it soon became impossible to see and I had to feel my way along the walls, frequently needing to skirt great masses of rock. I had gone a long way, firmly determined not to allow myself to imagine dangerous abysses or predatory beasts, when I caught sight of a thin ribbon of light. The light became brighter and I reached a broad expanse covered with rock fragments—evidence that the cave had been created by a landslide. At the far side, there were boulders piled one atop the other, allowing one to climb higher. I saw that, near the tallest rocks, there were carved stones similar to what we had seen on the buildings in the ancient city. Higher up, the light was blocked by the outlines of leafy branches. I stood there motionless, joyously contemplating the way out. A persistent sound like the buzzing of countless insects drew my attention. Looking through the opening that led to the jungle, I could see bees on the wing. The sun glinted off their bodies, giving them the brightness of live sparks.

I climbed up to the very top of the pile of boulders and discovered the back of the honeycombs: trickles of honey hanging in the half light, like tiny stalactites. I scooped out the hole, filled my cupped hands with honey, and raised it eagerly to my mouth. Its sweetness bore the fragrances of the jungle. And just as the songs of the birds, echoed by the water in the infinite calm of the night, had communicated to me a message of death, so the honey that I had gathered, along with the sight of the vegetation and the sun, made me certain that I was out of danger.

I feasted for some time. The hives were overflowing with honey, so I knew there must be any number of swarms of bees among the rocks. When my hunger was satisfied, I remembered my godfather. I gathered as much honey as I could, joining my two hands like a bowl, and made my way back through the narrow path as confidently as though I had done it many times before.

"Godfather, honey, food."

He was still delirious, but when I put the honey to his mouth he began to lick it avidly. He rose to his feet and, taking the honey eagerly from my hands, devoured the rest of it. Eating had restored his consciousness.

"Where did you get it from?"

"Godfather," I said, "I've found the way out. We must follow along the walls of the cave. At most, it's two hundred paces."

"Blessings on you, Miguel. Let us get out of here this minute."

"How do you feel?"

"Terrible, I swear by the devil and all his hosts. But I would rather be out of here before I feel even worse."

He leaned on my shoulder and slowly we entered the darkness. The journey through the cave took a long time. The ascent to the jungle level in the last cavern was also long and difficult, but finally we reached the outside. The bees hovered about as though welcoming us. We found ourselves near the first buildings of the city, just a stone's throw from a pyramidal structure.

I searched for a place where I could make my godfather comfortable, for he seemed on the verge of losing consciousness. I had to watch each step we took, since we were barefoot and risked being bitten by a poisonous snake.

CHAPTER XII

I found a good shelter in one of the stone dwellings alongside the pyramid. It was well preserved and would protect us from downpours. At first, the contrast between the light outside and the half shadow inside made it difficult to see the painted figures that covered the walls, but they slowly took on shape and color before my eyes.

There were depictions of human beings with piercing eyes, squatting on their heels, delicately sipping from small bowls, while others seemed to be dancing. The dancers were dressed in what were unmistakably jaguar skins, and the others had nothing on but loincloths, very much like those of the Indian peoples of my region. To one side, protected by an overhang, several female figures, dressed in long *huipiles*, stood watching the drinkers and the dancers. All around the images there were quadrangular and circular symbols which, strung together in long rows, represented perhaps the characters of some sort of writing. Presiding over all the paintings was a creature which looked like a gigantic bird with sharp claws and long, colored plumes.

Despite the darkness of the place and my scanty garments, I felt a mugginess that soon had me bathed in sweat. The smell of rotting leaves reminded me of a stable, and during the night a swarm of mosquitoes swooped down on us, waking us from our slumber with a start.

We stayed there two days. We fed ourselves on the honey and on some fruit I discovered nearby, but my godfather was feverish and mostly semiconscious. The wound looked even worse than it had before.

If by some chance my grandfather had been with us, he could have told me what herbs, among the endlessly diverse vegetation around us, were the ones that might cure my godfather. However, of all the knowledge of my Indian forebears, I have nothing left, save for their language. And it was then that I realized how unfair I had been regarding the traditions, customs, and knowledge of the peasants of my homeland, looking on all that with contempt when compared to what came from the Court in Castile. So, though I might be able to translate some fragment or other of Julius Caesar's eyewitness accounts of his war against the Gauls, I am unable to tell which leaves, when chewed, make a fever go down.

One night I dreamed that my godfather's horse had returned and was waiting at the entrance to our dwelling, alerting his master with a neigh that he was back. I woke up, but the only sound was that of the jungle, birdcalls and screechings amid the dense foliage. Yet I heard the neigh once again, and I hurried out, seeking its origin. The smell of firewood indicated that someone else was living among the ruins.

I heard the neighing again, and a murmur of voices, but I couldn't make out whether they were Christian or Indian. I went toward them: a series of stone pillars allowed me to draw closer with great caution. Though it was not possible to see who was talking, I was close enough to tell that the voices were speaking in the language of the Indians of that region. I was about to withdraw just as cautiously when I was pinned down by two Indians.

Like the Indians in the paintings in our shelter, these men wore loincloths and their black hair was tied back with a hairband. Their prominent aquiline nose was the main feature of their faces. They were no taller than I, nor were they very robust, yet they had pinned me to the ground.

They shouted, and from the other side of the pillars more Indians appeared, armed with lances and arrows. I was surrounded. But immediately thereafter I heard voices in a Christian tongue asking the reason for this disturbance, and finally the Sevillian, Juan García, appeared between the pillars. When he saw me, he jabbered a few words to the Indians in their language, and they let me go.

"I find you in a sea of troubles, my lad," he said. "What's happened to you? Where is your good godfather? And where is that girl, Lucía, the one with such pretty eyes?"

I heaved a sigh. This friendly encounter broke through my resolve and I almost burst into tears.

Finally I said: "My godfather is badly wounded. I fear for his life."

"Where is he?"

"Follow me," I said.

When we reached my godfather at the shelter, the Indians readied a stretcher and transported him to their campsite, where he was placed in a shed very much like the one that had served us as a refuge.

To my surprise, I discovered that, among the people at the campsite—several Indians and four Christians—were the twin damsels that I had first seen in chains in the camp of Captain Justino de Corcos. They were very pretty, with a darkish complexion and extraordinarily beautiful black eyes. They were small in stature, but graceful, and were wearing *huipiles*—one in red and the other in shades of blue—with embroidered edgings of birds and plants.

The two came to my godfather and looked at his wound. One spoke with Juan García and it took me a few moments to realize that she was using a rudimentary Castilian, pronounced in the fashion of the local language.

"Much fever. Much pus," she said.

The twins then made their way into the dense vegetation, accompanied by some Indians, for doubtless they still possessed the age-old knowledge of the art of healing. They ground the plants, mixed and boiled them together, and prepared poultices on small squares of cotton cloth. One of the twins scraped around the edges of the wound with a small jade knife and cleaned away the pus, then placed the poultice on it. Several of the men held my godfather down, for the treatment caused terrible pain. But at last he was prostrate again and fell fast asleep.

As we ate, Juan García told me that he and the other Christians in his party had made their escape from Captain Justino de Corcos's camp on the very day that we left, as preparations were being made for an attack on the Indian army that, according to news brought by the sentry who arrived at dawn, was drawing closer.

The captain had ordered the expeditionary party to take the two captive damsels with them, so as to put them to death within sight of the rebels; as their liberation was apparently the principal reason for the Indians' attack.

This capped our friend's indignation, as well as that of many other soldiers who thought the captain's cruelties despicable and who had taken pity on the two girls. They quickly decided to set them free, and taking advantage of the way the troops were scattered, some of the mutinous soldiers managed to flee the camp with them.

"Later on, we came across a small advance guard of the rebel Indians. Though hostile to start with, they became friendly when they recognized the two girls and realized that we were their liberators. We are now heading for their village. Among their own people, the twins are noble princesses and the Indians hold them in great esteem," he concluded.

On the following day I was unable to see any signs of

improvement in my godfather's condition, but Juan García told me that it was imperative for us to leave.

"We must not stay here any longer," he said. "The Indians say that we are at most two days' journey from the village. We'll take don Santiago with us. He'll be better taken care of there, and whatever we can do to cure him will be done."

CHAPTER XIII

The village was located in a place where the vast plain turns into gently rolling hills and the jungle, which is always dense in this region, becomes thicker and more inextricable. There had been an ancient city there also, now in ruins overgrown with vegetation.

Of the old settlement, only a large public square and two buildings on the square remained free of vegetation. One of the buildings was a pyramid—which was still in use as a temple—and opposite it was a high cylindrical tower crowned by a cupola with a number of openings. Nearby, in a clearing, was the settlement of the present-day villagers. Their houses were made of wattle and daub, roofed over with palm fronds.

Both the pyramid and the cylindrical tower were neatly

painted and no doubt had the same appearance they must have had when they were first built.

The pyramid was painted red and consisted of successive superimposed levels, like the floors of a building, the highest one surmounted by a room with a narrow door. Above the room was a stone summit decorated in polychrome reliefs. The various levels of the pyramid, up to the room at the top, were connected by a stairway that must have had more than eighty steps. I found out later that, in front of the narrow door of the topmost room, which is where sacrifices took place, a censer of copal was supposed to be permanently lighted, but it had been extinguished so as not to give any sign that might make the settlement easier to locate.

As for the cylindrical tower, it, too, was painted red, although its cupola was white and gleamed like silver.

As we approached the village, a group of children came out to meet us. From inside the dwellings came the sound of dough being vigorously kneaded for maize tortillas. At each door, women were grinding maize in metal vessels or stirring the contents of their cooking pots. Let loose in the village, turkeys were pecking among the puddles left from the last downpour.

Behind the village, in another expanse cleared of trees, there were terraces supported by stones where crops of maize, beans, tomatoes, and squash were grown. Men were toiling in the cultivated fields, clearing out the underbrush.

We Christians were assigned one of the huts, with a corral in back for the four horses on which my friend the

Sevillian and his comrades had escaped with the twins. We found my godfather stretched out on a straw mat, leaning back on cotton cushions. Shortly after that, one of the priests came to see him, dressed in a long tunic on which the dried blood of sacrifices seemed to form part of the fabric itself. He lit copal at my godfather's feet and recited long incantations, then made him drink several herb concoctions and placed new poultices on his wounds.

Despite all this, I did not see any sign of improvement in my godfather's condition. On the contrary, the approach of death seemed more and more obvious. He no longer spoke, and only his eyes gave any indication that he was still aware of anything.

Juan García told me that, according to the Indian healer, the wounded man might still recover. I clung to that possibility, though the thought that my godfather might die made me very sad. I lived through those days so lost in thought that I often came out of my absorption in surprise, having forgotten what I was doing and where I was. When I recovered my senses, I would as readily find myself at my godfather's side as in some distant part of the village, where I had gone, lost in thought, through the mere unpremeditated movement of my feet.

I came across the twin girls in the jungle during one of my solitary wanderings. We met near a pit similar to the one my godfather and I had found out about on that ill-starred occasion, but this one was much narrower and darker. I already knew that the Indians called these natural reservoirs *cenotes*. When they saw me, the twin sisters beamed, and the one who spoke Castilian showed me the contents of a little basket that she was carrying over her arm.

"Herbs and flowers to cure the wounded man," she said.

I did not reply.

"He is very ill, but he is going to get well," she added.

Then the other one spoke, but in a language closely resembling that of my mother's people. "He'll be cured, he'll be fine. You shouldn't worry; don't be afraid."

I looked at her in surprise.

"My sister knows the language of the bearded ones from the east through a maidservant," she said. "The maidservant was an Indian, but had spent time with the Spaniards before she came to us. I was brought up by a slave girl who came from my mother's part of the country. Ever since I was a baby, she spoke Nahuatl to me. I don't know Spanish, just as my sister doesn't know the language that I speak."

From that day on, the three of us fell into the habit of taking walks together to chat. The conversations, during which I would serve as interpreter for each of them, little by little became full of small secrets that I would share with each separately, for though I did my best to translate faithfully to the other the main points of what I said to her sister, the need to abbreviate forced me to resort to simplifications which, eliminating nuances or repeated references, gradually created two dialogues, to which I alone was a party.

I must say also that the sadness I had plunged into in those days, which I regarded as the last in my godfather's life, linked me to the two of them in a strange friendship paradoxically filled with happiness, in which our conversations came to have as great a place as bursts of laughter, embraces, and caresses. Being far removed from Christian customs, the girls expressed their affection for me very freely, leaving me full of confusion and embarrassment and even scruples, but at the same time arousing in me, with sensations never before felt, an inexpressible fascination with their beauty.

They told me the story of their people—the people who, countless years before, built the cities now lost to the jungle.

No one among them knew why their ancestors had abandoned their cities. They believed that time goes around in infinite circles, that it has no beginning and will have no end. And just as the same day is repeated every fifty-two years—a familiar concept to me from my mother's people—it is possible that at some time or other the days of that lost time will return, days in which their cities shone in all their splendor.

But they put no concrete hope on the return of that former glory, for an old maxim of their people counsels resignation and skepticism. I copied it down here because it struck me as the essence of what they told me and because it inspired me to reflect for a long while on its meaning:

Every moon, every year, every day, every wind passes by and continues on its way.
Likewise, all blood reaches its resting place, as it reaches its power and its throne.

The legends that they had heard since they were little girls evoked the glory of the olden days: the great buildings and their public squares and avenues triumphant over the jungle; the vast expanses of abundant crops; the reservoirs of water and the stone quarries; the people busying themselves constructing buildings and repairing the walls and roads.

They evoked the fairs and the markets where lengths of cloth, pottery and tools, candles and baskets were sold. They spoke of the precious objects that came from afar, in caravans: obsidian knives, jade figurines and symbols, fans and capes of feathers, and ocarinas whose sound reproduces the most mysterious plaints of the jungle. They also told of forgotten games, such as one that was played in a special theater, the players and their ball representative of other, far vaster games and movements.

The awareness of that splendor forever dimmed, of that brightness irredeemably darkened, had about it a melancholy that was a good match for my sorrow. At a time when I feared the imminent loss of my godfather—who, when I lacked a father, was one for me when I was a small boy—those stories of things gone forever, of things longed for through a vague memory, were like the warm embraces of the two sisters, a contradictory consolation.

They told me other stories as well. All of them, with elements common to the rural world but filled with fantastic happenings very much like the stories of other peoples, seemed to conceal meanings of which the storytellers themselves were unaware. What interested me most of all was the story of a dwarf who became king and through magic built one of the most beautiful cities of ancient times. Here is the story:

There was once a city whose governors for many a year lived under the shadow of a prophecy that the chief of their tribe would be overthrown by one who, not born of woman, would make the bell hidden beneath fire and earth ring.

On the outskirts of the city, in a tiny hut surrounded by plots of cultivated crops, lived an old woman who knew magic spells. Through her magic she spoke with the little hunchbacks who lived in the hills and roamed about at night amid the brambles.

The years went by and the old woman grew older and more exhausted. One day she felt that her death was imminent. But she did not want to die without a son, so she sought help from the little hunchbacks, who gave her an egg and told her to incubate it underground. The old woman did so, and in time a baby boy with the face of an old man was born from the egg, and he grew to be less than five feet tall.

The old woman was delighted and told everyone that the dwarf was her grandson. The dwarf, for his part, caused everyone to marvel at his wisdom.

But there was something that the dwarf did not know: and that was what the old woman was hiding in the hearth, in a place where she carefully piled up ashes, keeping watch to see that no one ever disturbed them.

The dwarf had the idea of pricking a tiny hole in the bottom of the vessel which his grandmother used to fetch water from the well, so that it would take a long time to fill and he could meanwhile discover the old woman's secret. And one day, as she lingered at the well filling her pitcher, the dwarf searched under the ashes and found a tiny golden bell.

He rang the bell and a tremendous peal resounded throughout the world. Everyone was afraid and wondered where it came from. The tribal chieftain was frightened, too, and sent forth his emissaries to locate the person who had produced the sound.

The emissaries traveled far and wide and finally found the dwarf, who showed them the magical bell. They took the dwarf to the city and brought him to the chieftain. But the chieftain had received advice from his counselors and had decided not to leave the throne without subjecting the dwarf to a number of tests.

First the chieftain asked him how many leaves were on the most ancient silk-cotton tree of the region. The dwarf reflected for a few moments and then answered in a confident voice, for he had been born with the knowledge of the number of leaves on the trees, of the feathers of birds, and of the hairs on the head of a human being. The figure was large and complicated, but a great black parrot came out from among the branches of the silk-cotton tree and fluttered about over the heads of the many people present, affirming that the dwarf had given the right figure.

For the second test, the chieftain was to break, one by one, all the coconuts that would fit in a basket over the dwarf's head, using an enormous stone mace. The dwarf agreed to the test, after making the chieftain promise to undergo the same test if he, the dwarf, survived. The following day the people all stared in amazement as up to twenty times twenty coconuts were broken over the dwarf's head with an enormous stone mace. The dwarf never stopped smiling during the ordeal, for the old woman who had brought him up had hidden a magic shell under his hair which made him invulnerable to the blows.

Having now become rivals, the dwarf and the chieftain took part in the third and last test: each would make a figure in his own image, which would then be passed through the flames of an immense bonfire. The figure that was not destroyed would indicate who the winner was.

Eager to ensure that he would be the winner, the chieftain produced three figures: one of wood, another of stone, and a third of metal. Once in the fire, the wooden one burned, the stone one split open, and the metal one melted, whereupon his failure was much commented upon.

The dwarf, for his part, modeled a figure out of damp clay and the flames, instead of destroying it, fired it, hardening it. The figure was of the dwarf wearing a cape of feathers, a great headdress of intricate knots and leaves, and a jade necklace, and holding a little golden bell in one hand.

The dwarf was proclaimed the winner. It was announced that on the following day the dwarf would declare himself chieftain of the tribe, after building a city worthy of the new kingdom. But before that happened, the dwarf demanded that the old chieftain submit to the test of having all the coconuts in a basket broken over his head. The first blow of the mace ended his life. As for the city, on the following day it appeared in full splendor before the astonished eyes of the people, with buildings such as had never before been seen. The dwarf lived in the tallest one of all, and from there he governed for many *katuns*. His people were children of the moon, whereas the children of the previous chieftain had been children of the sun.

There was a great intimacy between the two sisters and me, when there seemed to be a slight improvement in my godfather's condition. My sorrow gradually turned to optimism and I began to experience a curiosity about everything around about me, becoming all the greater after I learned of the long-gone grandeur of the ancient cities that the jungle had devoured.

One day, rummaging about in the hut where the Indians stored the booty from their forays against the Spaniards, I found writing materials and began setting down an account of my adventures. I wrote during the time that the two sisters, along with the other villagers, were obliged to attend to tasks in the fields and in the kitchens. I helped out by carrying wood, but at midmorning I was free to do whatever I pleased.

I gradually regained a taste for writing as my godfather convalesced. A few days after the beginning of what would seem to be his full recovery, I became absorbed in this task for hours at a time.

CHAPTER XIV

My work as a writer increased, for when the sorcerer found out what I was doing, he asked me, through the twins, to write down what he dictated, using the characters of the Spanish alphabet to form the words of his own language. He said that the conquistadors were destroying all the Indian writings that fell into their hands. Hence, it would be more and more difficult for the knowledge handed down by the ancestors to survive if it was written in the characters of the original language.

In answer to my questions, the sisters told how the Spanish priests order old books to be burned whenever they come across them. The books are made of bleached tree bark, and instead of turning one after the other, the pages fold over, one atop the other, and are enclosed between two panels to preserve them. I have seen the one the sorcerer possesses and it is quite beautiful, with figures of people and birds and plants painted in a great variety of colors and surrounded by strange signs, which are words set down according to the old way of writing.

Apparently, the Christian priests want to destroy these books because the work of the devil may be preserved in such writings. This filled me with distress, since copying the account that the sorcerer had might perhaps mean collaborating in the perpetuation of abominable knowledge. But for lack of anyone with better judgment than mine to enlighten me as to what I ought to do, and filled, moreover, with curiosity, I decided to do as he wished, devoting to this task the morning hours I once spent gathering wood for the village.

And so each morning I climb the stairs of the pyramid, up to the temple. Just outside the door there is a stone altar in the form of a youth, half reclining, his torso and knees raised, who is holding a flat receptacle in his hands. Not far from him, in the shade of the temple, I sit down in front of a makeshift desk fashioned from planks, and write in Spanish characters what the priest dictates to me in his language.

When it rains, we go inside the building, a gloomy place which, to judge by the stains from smoke and perhaps blood, must have been the setting of countless sacrifices. The door, the only opening, affords a view of the jungle's horizon, hemmed in by an endless line of trees.

The two sisters sit on either side of me, helping me when I'm in doubt and translating the words of the sorcerer, who speaks very slowly and with his eyes closed.

First I transcribed the story of their gods. Since my childhood I had heard the friars speak of the one true God, but these accounts reminded me of the beliefs of my mother's people. They were like the fables or tales that are told at a gathering in the evening, before people go off to bed, and I found nothing diabolical or sinful about them.

The sorcerer told that the entire earth rests on the back of a huge lizard that floats on the surface of a lagoon. Above the earth rises the sky, a pyramid laid out in thirteen levels, each one governed by a god. Underneath the earth there are nine levels or worlds, governed by the lords of the night. At the beginning of time there was a war between the gods of the celestial realm and the lords of the underworld.

The sorcerer described the colors of the four directions of the earth: the white of the north, the yellow of the south, the red of the east, and the black of the west. In each of the four directions there is one of the four great trees: the Great White Mother Ceiba, the Great Yellow Mother Ceiba, the Great Red Mother Ceiba, and the Great Black Mother Ceiba. Each one presides over the animate and inanimate beings corresponding to its respective color: the stones and the earth, animals and vegetables, birds and insects. The four rain gods are also found in the four directions of the world. And in the center of the world, where all points and all regions of the universe meet, the Great Green Mother Ceiba rises.

The priest also told of the reigns of the First Time, of the Second Time, and of other successive times. Times are born and die, are created and destroyed, arise and are lost. And in one of these times the gods, wanting to be adored, tried to get animals to speak, but did not succeed.

So they made men: at first out of earth and mud, but water dissolved them; and then out of wood, but these were without reason and understanding and the gods did away with them by means of a great flood, and their descendants were the monkeys of the jungle. Finally, the gods created men out of corn. They made their flesh, their innards, and their limbs out of white and yellow corn.

I went on to transcribe the ancient stories of the first heroes, of the founders of bloodlines and family trees: where they came from, what roads they followed, beside which *cenotes* they rested on their journeys on foot, how they gradually peopled and brought order to the land and named the places on it. How, finally, they gave rise to other peoples and other means of organization. Predominant over everyone else were the sorcerers, who studied the sky, and the warriors, knights who belonged to one of the two great orders: that of the eagle, symbolizing the rising sun, and that of the jaguar, symbolizing the setting sun.

Then the sorcerer described time and its measurement, and though many of the concepts are identical to those of my Indian forebears, I was amazed at the variety of eras into which time was divided and by the diversity of names used to tell one from the other. I faithfully transcribed the names and made sketches, according to his instructions, of the circles and figures that represented the passage of time and its subdivisions.

In addition to the names for each day, which they called *kin*, and to the names for each of thirteen successive days, they had names for periods of twenty days, which they called *uinal*, and for the year, which they called *tun*. This last was made up of eighteen months of twenty days each, to which were added another five days that were regarded as ill-fated or ominous. There were also names for periods of twenty years, which they called *katun*.

All of this sounded familiar to me. But they also had a name for a period of twenty *katuns*, which they called a *baktun*, and for that of twenty *baktuns*, which they called a *pictun*, and for that of twenty *pictuns*, and so on, till they arrived at a unit of time that I am almost unable to imagine: the *alautun*, which is made up of twenty-three million days.

The *katuns* formed cycles within time, and people were so familiar with their passage, which conformed to that of the stars in the sky, to the waxing and waning of the moon, and to the rising and setting of the sun, that they had a perfect knowledge of the best dates for sowing crops and for harvesting, for hunting and fishing, for obtaining, in short, everything essential for their subsistence. And in this manner they tamed the jungle and cultivated dry, scarcely fertile land that was mostly stones. They worked in harmony with the rhythms that determine the rains and germination, managing to feed multitudes of people.

Moreover, they worked only half the days of the year, devoting the other half to festivals. There was the feast for making new gods—clay idols; for honoring the rain gods; for lighting the first fire; for putting fire out with water; for commemorating the most ancient of the founding heroes; for the beginning of the new year, when they replaced all their household pottery with new pieces; for fishermen; for beekeepers; for ensuring the growth of children . . . and many others like them. And at all of them the villagers ate and drank their fill, danced, and made merry together.

I also copied down many of their laws and their punishments, some of them very cruel, such as killing the condemned man by dropping a huge stone on him.

The sorcerer then dictated to me the chronicle of the arrival of the *tsules*, which was their name for the conquistadors. According to their system of reckoning time, it was on one of the days called Ahau, the eleventh. And though the splendor of their cities had vanished long before, the arrival of the Spaniards, according to the sorcerer, marked the final decadence of his people and the beginning of servitude for the descendants of that wise and glorious tribe. The beginning of tribute, the beginning of plundering.

And that very old man, with disheveled, dirty hair and wrinkled, trembling hands, voiced his laments amid tears, like a little boy.

CHAPTER XV

My godfather had grown so much better that, though his voice was still very feeble, he was able to converse; he also began to eat with gusto.

"I was on the point of departing from this vale of tears, Miguel."

I was overjoyed at seeing his recovery.

"How is everything?" he asked.

I told him in detail about our ups and downs since we got out of the *cenote*. I also told him that I had found a set of writing equipment and was setting down the story of our adventure.

I didn't tell him about my work as copyist of the stories of the Indians, fearing his reproaches; but on one of the mornings when the sorcerer and the two sisters came for me, he was awake and asked me what they had wanted. I promised to tell him when I came back and he did not forget. At midday, when I returned to the hut, he repeated his question.

"I'm writing an account dictated by that elder of the tribe whom they call Chilam," I replied. "I write down, in Castilian, the words he says in his language. The two young women help out with what they know, so that my copy will be as faithful as possible."

"What does this account consist of?"

I shrugged, on the point of saying that I didn't know. But then I told the truth. "It tells the story of the creation of man, according to these people's beliefs, and what gods their ancestors worshipped, and who the founders of their ancient empires were."

My godfather raised himself as high as he was able to and said to me in a grave voice: "Miguel, my son. Hasn't it entered your mind that you may be an instrument for perpetuating superstitions and idolatries? Haven't you considered that perhaps you are recording in your own hand, in written words, falsehoods of the devil and the most wicked acts of deceit imaginable?"

I was silent for a few moments. Then I said: "Yes, the thought has occurred to me, Godfather. But they saved your life with their knowledge of plants that heal and their spirit of generosity. Moreover, the tales they tell me come from long ago, and I find in them no offense to the name of God or of the Virgin, or anything to discredit our Holy Mother Church."

He gave signs of great doubt, but did not press the point. Moreover, very little time remained before my work would be finished, for after another long list of laments, the sorcerer—who was born cross-eyed and became even more so when he made his pronouncements—said that his account was coming to an end and in his most solemn voice began to dictate to me prophecies for the twenty *katuns* that would follow the time we were living in.

I understood almost nothing. The old man described each of the coming *katuns* in a brief paragraph. References to the old gods and the names of the stars were intermingled with bitter omens of things to come. For the very last *katun* he prophesied a cataclysm, a tremendous rain, an unending downpour, a deluge reminiscent of the one that, according to his faith, had destroyed the lineage of primordial men and one of the very earliest times.

His prophecies ended, the priest lay exhausted on the altar in front of the temple door. The twin sisters asked me for the final pages of my transcript, which I handed to them.

"You may keep the writing kit," the one who spoke Castilian said. "It is our gift to you for your work."

I thanked them and went down the steps of the pyramid. The village was noticeably animated at that time, for some of the Indian warriors who had participated in the attack on the camp of don Justino de Corcos had returned not long before. They did not tell of a total victory, for apparently the Indian warriors had been defeated once again by the Spaniards and many had been taken captive, but they did bring the news that the enemy captain had died in one of the skirmishes. The Indians said that the captain was strangled to death when he fell off his horse and became entangled in his own reins. They attributed a special symbolic significance to this incident, which in a sense turned their defeat into an important victory.

On learning this news, the Christians in the village—who had become more gloomy with each passing day—took heart again, for now that the captain, greatly feared by one and all, was dead, nothing stood in the way of their return to the army of the Adelantado. They could justify to the Adelantado their having strayed from their campsite by citing the scattering of the troops, which was true, and the difficulty of finding their way back, in addition to the attack of the Indian rebels—a convincing story that would make their flight seem to be an attempt to save the two girls from being put to death.

I found out all this when I returned to the shelter with my writing kit. The Sevillian was talking with my godfather, who was now able to walk, with the aid of a crutch. The Sevillian was telling him that the four Christians would leave immediately, the next day or the following one, and that he would accompany them, unless we had need of him.

"We, too, will leave in your company," my godfather said, "if you will allow me the use of one of your mounts during some stretches of the journey, for I still feel too weak to travel entirely by foot."

I was taken aback. Suddenly I realized that I had never really thought about leaving the village. I gave an inward start that shook my very being, and the twins came to my mind with particular intensity. I knew then that having to leave them would be a wrenching experience. The expression on my face must have shown my state of mind, for both men were staring at me.

"Do you have something to say, Miguel? What's the matter?"

Both men were in rags and tatters and their beards were unkempt. I imagined the series of military camps that would mark our route, whatever trail we decided to take, and saw images of war and destruction. Yet in that village the peace of another time reigned—the tranquil customs of a life organized in the knowledge that it is a part of the movement that makes the evening star rise up and the sun go down.

Furthermore, my friendship with the sisters had become essential to me, as nothing else ever had. I was smitten with their beauty: their faces, the sound of their voices, the purity of their skin, the softness of their hands and limbs. It was also fascinating that I could never tell the two apart. After spending so much time with them, however, I suspected the sisters understood both the Castilian and the Indian tongues, and that the little secrets I thought I shared with only one or the other were no such thing; that they alone possessed the key to their secrets.

I didn't answer. I turned around abruptly and quickly left the shack, heading toward the jungle, where I might hide my disappointment.

I went to the *cenote*, which during the early evening hours was a peaceful place surrounded by birds and teeming with butterflies. It was possible to descend to the surface of the water by means of a large basket connected to strong braided ropes, to a long platform made of planks which also served to hold water pitchers during a rain, and where the Indians left their clothes when they bathed.

The two sisters were swimming in the *cenote*. On other afternoons I had gone swimming with them among the strange blind whitish fish, which at certain hours came to the surface, the inhabitants perhaps of very dark submerged caves. The sisters bathed as naked as the day their mother brought them into the world, but there was such an innocence to them when they showed themselves this way that I never felt the least embarrassment and I myself stripped naked, swimming with them in those waters as though the three of us had retained the innocence of our first parents in the Garden of Eden.

They caught sight of me and waved from the water, urging me to come down. But I stayed at the top, watching their playful movements in the water. Their bodies were as alike as their faces. The thought came to me then that perhaps the disappointment I felt, and my distress at having to part with them, came from my having fallen in love with them, as happened to the heroes in books of chivalry in the course of their adventures.

I had never felt like this before, and I analyzed my feelings with amazement. In me there were the same desires toward each: to remain at their side forever, to listen to them and to gaze on them with the greatest of pleasures, to feel the heat of their bodies and their fragrance, which came from the scent of flowers and aromatic herbs. And the confusion of my feelings increased, for knights-errant, as far as I know, do not fall in love with two damsels at the same time. And yet I felt then and still feel in my heart today a great love for both of them and the same longing for both, without any distinction.

Dressed, the twins finally climbed up the cliff face, greeting me with peals of laughter. One was named Ix Cuzam and the other Ix Mucuy, but because I was never able to tell them apart, even now I wonder if the sisters answered to either name indiscriminately.

"I'd like to speak with you," I said.

We sat in the ruins of a building, on an immense carved stone which had perhaps been an enormous pillar at one time. Darkness was falling, and the echoes and murmurs of the jungle seemed more intense.

"The Spaniards want to leave," I said. "My godfather wants to leave with them. But I am going to stay."

I think that as I spoke I mixed together my two languages and the one I am learning here. But the sisters appeared to understand me.

"I don't want to leave you," I added. "My heart cannot part from you."

They were sitting on either side of me. They looked at me without a smile, their faces grave and sad. They took my hands in theirs. One of them spoke in the old language of my mother: "Listen. We don't want you to be sad. But you must leave with them."

The other sister spoke in Castilian and our conversation took on the usual multilingual sound of all our chats.

"We are very fond of you, too; our hearts also ache because you are going away. But this is not your rightful place. And we will not always be with you. We serve a people spread far and wide."

"I will go wherever the two of you go. I will safeguard you and assist you."

"The gods made us equal in our mother's womb and that, which was once considered ominous, is interpreted by our people as a good omen in these fateful times. We cannot think of any other way of life than to follow the designs of our wise men, of our Chilames and Kines. We must be completely free and completely on our own."

"But I could be a part of your entourage. I could be just another warrior among your people."

"You, too, must fulfill your destiny, follow those who are yours, complete the journey that was your reason for leaving home."

Then the twins began to intone a long peroration that sounded like a prayer. They did not translate it for me, nor did I ask them to. When they finished, we remained silent till the last light of day was gone. I felt truly wretched.

CHAPTER XVI

Our departure date was finally settled on and the cacique of the village announced that we would be provided with food, as well as with garments and footwear from the booty that the Indians had taken in their battles with our troops. But we would not be allowed to take any weapons save a crossbow for hunting. He also said that the village would offer a great feast in honor of our departure.

The feast took place on the evening before we left. The sorcerer, the cacique, the two sisters, a number of warriors, and we Christians seated ourselves on the steps of the pyramid. As part of the feast, dances and spectacles were to take place in the public square between the two towering ancient buildings. The villagers seated themselves lower down. It was almost dark and the site of the festivities was illuminated by a multitude of torches and braziers.

First came the sounds of the drums, whistles, and ocarinas, then a beautiful, intricate dance in which the dancers formed a circle and stepped out of it at intervals, two by two, without breaking the rhythm. As part of the dance, they threw lances to each other, tossing and catching them with such dexterity that no one would be hurt.

Then they staged, to our wonderment, the imprisonment of the two sisters, their sentencing to death, and their rescue by the Sevillian and his comrades. The faces of the actors were painted red and only the movements and gestures of their bodies indicated which role each was playing in the spectacle, which had us enthralled.

At the end came an abundant banquet of stewed vegetables and venison and game birds, accompanied by a tasty foaming drink made of maize and ground cocoa that reminded me of the tang of the festive beverage served at my mother's house. There was also a strong wine made from water, honey, and the root of a certain plant.

There was great merriment and the Sevillian sang songs from Spain with great charm. One of them went:

Only an oak tree, an oak tree,
only an oak tree.

I was off, on a pilgrimage, Mother dearest.
To be more devout, I went by myself.
I took a different route, I left the road I'd been following,
and found myself lost in the wilderness.

At the foot of an oak tree I lay down to sleep.
At midnight I woke, ever so uneasy,
to find myself in the arms of my loved one.
With a heavy heart I saw the dawn break.
Blessed be the pilgrimage for love's sake!

Then two of the soldiers who, along with the Sevillian, had rescued the twins, danced the jota and sang. The Indians were delighted with them and, even though they did not understand the words, took pleasure in the sound and the rhythm of the songs.

Toward the end of the evening there were many drunken revelers and quite a few altercations, though the women did their best to calm their inebriated spouses and steer them home.

By then it was very late. We bade farewell to everyone and started climbing down the steps of the pyramid to get to bed, when the twins begged me to wait. I followed them up to the temple at the very top of the pyramid. From there, the jungle gleamed in the starlight. A lantern lit the inside of the temple, where the sorcerer who had dictated everything that I had set down in Castilian characters was waiting.

The ancient Chilam spoke slowly, in a cracked voice, and the sisters served as his interpreters. "Our Chilam would like to thank you for having put his words into writing. He says that because of you much wisdom and many prophecies will be known in the time to come, when our people learn to set down in symbols what is said, as you do."

I bowed my head as a sign of courtesy for his kindness.

He spoke again, handing a small packet to the sisters. One of them addressed me thus: "He says that, although the blood of the *tsules* courses in your veins, you are also of the maize lineage and must render justice to what is yours without fail. He says never to forget it."

"I won't forget."

"As a token of friendship, he would like you to have a seal that will be of use to you in seeking aid from our brothers, wherever you may have need of it. Even though before the arrival of the *tsules* our different lineages that are spread throughout the land were enemies and rivals, those opposed today to the domination of the *tsules* are brothers in spirit."

It was a small kerchief full of hemp, with a solid object within. I took it in my hands and again bowed my head as a sign of respect.

"I will use it should the need arise, and I thank you with all my heart."

We left the old man and walked down the steps in silence. The public square was empty and the village had regained its usual silence.

"You know," I said to the sisters, "at dawn, when I leave you both, it will be as though I am torn apart, as though a piece of me is being ripped away. I have never felt like this before. Not even when I left my mother."

They did not answer, but drew apart a few paces, until they were at the edge of the dim light cast by the last torches. They spoke a few words of farewell and suddenly they disappeared in the darkness without my even hearing the sound of their footsteps.

I never saw them again. When we left, the village was

in silence, no doubt sleeping off the general drinking that had accompanied the feast.

My godfather, the Sevillian, and another man rode mules. The other two beasts carried the bundles of food, pottery vessels, and camp equipment. The rest of us proceeded on foot, accompanied by an Indian who would point us in the right direction to reach the Adelantado's camp.

Dawn broke and the jungle burst into life, but I walked along downhearted, completely absorbed in my feeling of loss. Then someone at my side spoke. It was the Sevillian, who had dismounted from his mule.

"Miguel," he said. "You musn't be so dispirited. *Sursum corda.*"

I sighed, shrugging my shoulders.

"Look, lad," he went on. "You will flirt with and court many a young lady and be enthralled by many a pretty face."

I looked at him, surprised that he knew my secret, and I'm sure my cheeks turned red. He clapped me on the back. "Which one did you like best?" And he burst out laughing. Then, not waiting for my answer, he went on: "Cupid's wounds are painful but seldom fatal. It is human to feel the pain, but also human to get over it. I'll tell you about the first time I fell in love and was sent packing, like you. You'll see that with the years such memories turn out to be sweet rather than bitter."

He went on chatting, telling me this or that tale of his love affairs, and by midday my spirits were more or less restored. Though the memory of the twins still makes my heart ache, I promised myself that when I do think of them, the bitterness of our parting will be replaced by memories of the happy moments we shared.

Darkness is now falling and we have camped in a clearing in the jungle, under the shelter of a ceiba tree that is at least a hundred years old. I always carry my writing kit with me and today I have been writing for a long time. The supply of paper that was in the kit is running out and I don't know how I'll get more so as to go on with my account.

I want to put in writing the fact that what the sorcerer gave me was a small round jade stone with a hole in the middle, carved to resemble the indistinct profile of a bird. The kerchief full of hemp, in which the stone was wrapped, has painted on it one of the symbols that are repeated in the stone bas-reliefs on the ancient buildings and in the paintings on the walls of their rooms.

CHAPTER XVII

I no longer remember how many days it took us to reach don Francisco de Montejo's camp. I know that it was longer than we had foreseen and that we attributed the delay to the circuitous routes which the Indian guide had us take, no doubt to disorient us concerning the location of his village. But finally he pointed us toward the northeast and before leaving told us that one more day's journey in that direction would take us to one of the white roads built in ancient times. That road would lead us to the age-old sacred city of Ti Coh—abandoned today like all the others—where the Adelantado had set up his main camp.

The camp of the Adelantado don Francisco de Montejo was situated on a vast plain, free of vegetation and underbrush, near an enormous expanse of ruins. As we came closer, we could see, organized into crews and under the command of soldiers, a great number of Indians removing stones from the immense old buildings for transport elsewhere.

The men at the guard post promptly allowed us to enter the camp, although they ordered us to place ourselves immediately at the orders of the camp commander. The camp is huge and well fortified, built in the manner of the huts of the natives. It has a number of permanent buildings, too, such as a church with a bell tower, and a residence for the Adelantado. My godfather led us all to the church first, to say a prayer of thanksgiving for our safe arrival. We then sought out the camp commander.

After hearing the account of the Sevillian and the other soldiers, the camp commander assigned them their place in the militia. As for my godfather and me, he said he would ask don Francisco de Montejo to grant us an audience—he would probably accept us into his militia if we wished to enlist.

We were received by the Adelantado the following morning in his residence, which consisted mainly of a great hall. Large sheets of paper were scattered all over the wooden floor.

My godfather gave a detailed account of who we were and how, by chance, we had ended up in the Adelantado's camp. My godfather vehemently denounced the conduct of the man in charge there—apparently the adjutant of the Adelantado himself—who, after robbing us of everything we had, tried to kill us.

The Adelantado, don Francisco de Montejo, is much

younger than my godfather. He is not very tall, but his looks inspire respect, perhaps because of his meticulous, courtly attire. He did not seem very surprised by the news we brought him.

"Are you referring to the bachelor-at-arms Juan de Simancas?"

"That's the very fellow I mean. Aided by two of his servants, he robbed me of my horses and everything of value that I had with me. He stole documents attesting to the appointment given me by His Majesty, and left me for dead, after forcing me into one of the great pits found hereabouts. My body bears the scar of an arrow which, at his order, was meant to kill me when I was defenseless. It was only through a miracle that my godson and I escaped with our lives."

He undid his shirt and showed the scar, which did not look as though it had healed properly.

"I know now who these persons are, my lord don Francisco," one of the Adelantado's counselors said. "The men who arrived with a reserve corps reported that the bachelor-at-arms Simancas and some of his men had parted company with the rest somewhere along the way, to look for some ruins."

"The bachelor-at-arms took me in by trickery. He separated us from the others to carry out his treachery with impunity, as far as possible from the troops and from my companions," my godfather explained.

"Were your companions a black servant and a young Indian girl?" the counselor asked.

"Yes," I exclaimed, unable to contain myself. "Where are they now?"

The counselor told us that, in view of our delay in arriving, a patrol had been sent out to various ruins, but because no one knew what city the bachelor had taken us to, the search was very difficult, for the provinces are full of old, abandoned settlements. Because the patrols had not been able to locate us, it was concluded that one of the bands of rebel Indians might have taken us prisoner. As for Rubén and Lucía, after days of waiting, they decided to search for us themselves; they headed south one day, retracing the route that had brought them there, and no one had heard from them since.

The Adelantado, a proud man, said that that bachelor-at-arms was a disloyal servant; his disappearance had coincided with the uncovering of dishonest and corrupt practices of which he was doubtless guilty. He declared that any misdeeds were solely the doings of the bachelor-at-arms and that he, the Adelantado, would not be responsible for any claims for recompense or retribution. But he gave us his assurance that he would do whatever he could to arrest the bachelor-at-arms and his band of malefactors. Written orders for their arrest would be sent immediately to the camps and garrisons. Finally, he offered to take us into his armed forces.

"But if that is not your wish, I shall not object to your staying on in the camp for some days as my guests."

We took our leave, accompanied by the counselor, who wanted to show us the site of the future city. The Adelantado wished the official dedication to take place on a date with some significance, the next Epiphany of Our Lord perhaps. According to what the counselor told us, the Adelantado spent most of his time concerned with projects for the city. He was making plans for the central cathedral, as well as the town hall, the hospital, and other public buildings. There were plans for the streets and public squares and for the location of public services, as well as the sites of the dwellings of the future residents—according to their status—and those reserved as grants from His Majesty. All these were traced on those sheets of large-sized paper that we had seen spread out on the floor of his residence.

The counselor said that don Francisco de Montejo was so impetuous by nature that not only was he preparing an account of the residents who would be members of the first town council, and those who would assume the posts of magistrates, aldermen, scribes, and bailiffs, but had also begun to draw up a first draft of the ordinances by which the future population would be governed. He had even submitted a request to His Majesty for the privilege of a coat of arms to ennoble the city and distinguish it from all others.

The demolition of the ancient buildings, at which crews of Indian workers labored, was for the specific purpose of providing materials for the construction of the new buildings.

"It's a shame that such beautiful works are being destroyed," I ventured to say.

The counselor, whose name was don Gonzalo Méndez, was silent for a few moments.

"Look, my boy," he finally said. "It is true that these buildings are beautiful, but it is also true that they are remnants of a grandeur that in the end was forced to submit to us. The Indians must see that our greatness and power are replacing their forebears' and merit their own settlements and public buildings. Don't forget, many of these Indian buildings were temples where the worship of the devil took place, along with the abominable practice of human sacrifice."

"It saddened me, too, that the very beautiful city of Mexico should be destroyed," my godfather added, emerging from the silence that had come over him after our audience with the Adelantado. "But the domination of the Indian empire necessarily meant the overshadowing and even the extinction of their symbols and customs."

"That's how it is in this business of conquest," the counselor said, "and the great conquerors of antiquity were no different—Alexander, for instance, when he destroyed Thebes, or Scipio when he razed Carthage, or Titus Jerusalem."

We ended up establishing a good relationship with the counselor, don Gonzalo Méndez, for at one point in our conversation it came out that he had been the comrade and friend of don Sabino Ordás, one of my godfather's uncles and a man of letters whom don Gonzalo had known in Italy.

He invited us to take our midday meal at his lodgings and spoke to us in confidence, about the conquest of Yucatan, which had lasted for so many years and had led to such bloodshed by both Christians and Indians. The first Adelantado, the father of the current one, spent eight fruitless years in the effort, and his son devoted more than three to the same undertaking, though with better luck—but now this venture was being eclipsed by the conquering of Peru, where gold and silver seemed to flow from inexhaustible lodes. Many Christians were heading there, since in the steaming jungles of Yucatan there was neither gold nor silver. Don Gonzalo said that, in view of the fierce resistance of the Indians and the dearth of Christians to control them, everything might well be lost again.

"Doubtless the bachelor-at-arms is heading for Peru," he commented.

"It's the devil that's taking him there, with my name, my credentials, and my money," my godfather exclaimed. "But the one who dances pays the piper, although it is also true that he with no shame seldom gets the blame."

"However, Peru is very unruly these days," the counselor went on. "After don Diego de Almagro was garroted, following a trial that wound up filling two thousand folios, the quarrels between the Spaniards there are more heated than ever."

The friendship and trust of don Gonzalo Méndez made those days very pleasant for us as well as useful, because of his good influence on the Adelantado, who, in my opinion, would not have moved his little finger to help us had it depended on him alone.

My godfather was uncertain what route would be best to follow, for though his prime considerations were the recovery of his credentials and revenge on the bachelor—this last involving our honor—my arguments that we ought first to try to find Lucía and Rubén seemed to him valid. Doubtless both of them, the girl especially, were trying to locate us and their determination might lead them into danger. It simply would not be right for us to leave without making every effort to unite our original party.

But we had absolutely no means to do this. My godfather spoke to don Gonzalo Méndez, who offered us whatever we needed; he lent us two good mounts, which we were to send back from the last garrison before embarking for Nombre de Dios. He also gave us clothes and provisions, a sword and two crossbows.

He was very short of money, so he was unable to give us very much; but he was able to get the Adelantado to sign a letter of introduction addressed to any ship's captain that we might encounter. It urged the captain to transport us with our cargo to the Royal Tribunal of Panama—where we were to be highly placed officials—with the assurance that this institution would pay for the costs of our passage.

And so, after bidding our generous friend farewell, we began our journey fairly well equipped and in good spirits. Our plan was to head south again, keeping our ears open for any news of Lucía and Rubén. Along our route, the territory was completely pacified; we passed farmhouses and hamlets with churches built in the Christian manner. The rainy season was ending and the sun was scorching hot, even in the shade of trees we sought out. My godfather and I traveled side by side.

"So you see now that God's grip is tight but doesn't strangle, Miguel," my godfather said. "After much travail, here we are alive and wagging our tails, continuing on our way as though nothing had happened. The only thing missing now is meeting up with our faithful Rubén and our charming Lucía. And then, I swear by the nails on Christ's hands, we will find that Simancas fellow, too, a ne'er-do-well and a scoundrel; we'll give him his just deserts, we'll recover what's ours, we'll arrive at our destination, and when we take up our life in our manor house or our palace, we will think that all these worries have been nothing but chaff in the wind. But as a wise Arab once said, the good part isn't living but having lived and being able to tell about it."

I said nothing in reply, but I felt a sense of joy and relief knowing that I had my godfather back, down to the last hair on his head, after coming so close to losing him.

CHAPTER XVIII

In the late afternoon of the first day, we came across a farm, protected by a palisade, on the edge of the jungle. We were received by the owner, a rich encomendero—a Spanish colonist who had been given Indian laborers by His Majesty—who told us his land was more fertile than we could possibly imagine. He had no fear of the Indians, for those who were native to the region had accepted their servitude, following the example of their caciques, and collaborated peacefully in the expansion and improvement of the colonists' land grants.

When we told him about Rubén and Lucía, he said he remembered them perfectly, for the black man and the Indian girl dressed in the Spanish manner made an unusual pair.

He said they were in search of certain persons, among them the bachelor-at-arms Simancas, a man well known for his ruthlessness. He also said that the day Rubén and Lucía stopped at the farm, some soldiers had also passed by who said they had seen the bachelor recently, but much farther east, and that he had with him only his two servants and seemed in a hurry to get on with whatever mission he had been given. On hearing this, Rubén and Lucía had decided to head east also, and had started out immediately, without waiting for another day to dawn.

We went on our way when dawn had barely broken, following a path that no doubt was frequently used for transportation and communication among the conquistadors. At midmorning we passed a military patrol, and at midday we met up with several merchants traveling together in a caravan, who in answer to our questions informed us that we were close to a settlement of friendly Indians.

Just outside the village was a shack which served as an inn, run by a Christian, where we took lodgings for the night. Three Franciscan friars were also there for the night, and before long my godfather struck up a conversation with them.

The friars told us that they were on their way to México–Tenochtitlán, on foot and without any other help than that of a few loyal Indians who served them as *tamemes*. They were going to visit the Viceroy don Antonio de Mendoza, known by everyone as a just and capable governor, to put before him their most serious complaints, which the Adelantado don Francisco de Montejo did not wish to, or was not able to, address.

The friars said that teaching the Christian doctrine—the principal aim of the Conquest, as was common knowledge—required not only patience on the part of the teachers and attention on that of the catechumens, but also time to explain and translate all its points and reasons. But the encomenderos—like the military—looked with contempt on this work. For the Indians to attend catechism classes, they had to stop working in the fields and serving in the military camps; and this dearth of younger Indians available for labor had greatly annoyed the encomenderos and the soldiers.

The friars voiced their most unfavorable opinion of the encomenderos. "They are cruel people and disinclined to respect either laws or ordinances," the youngest friar said. "The farther away they feel they are from the King, the more they do and undo, with neither bit nor bridle."

"May God forgive me," another friar added, "but the example they set is not a Christian one. Many of them have their houses full of women, like Moorish harems. They behave like lords and masters of these territories, treating the Indians like beasts of burden."

In their sermons at Mass, the friars would reproach the encomenderos for their conduct. The encomenderos were deeply offended by this and began to forbid the Indians to attend catechism classes, whereupon their relations with the friars deteriorated even further.

"Just last Sunday night, those tyrants perpetrated their worst evil: they burned down our monastery, and our church along with it. We lost everything, for it was built of wood and straw. And a good friar, Toribio de Villalpando, perished in the fire, along with six Indian servants."

My godfather couldn't believe his ears. "How can you be sure they were the ones responsible?" he asked.

"Because they had been riding on horseback around and around the monastery all day, to keep people from attending Mass, all the while shouting insults. When night fell, we shut ourselves inside, as a precaution against what might happen. Then, with absolute impunity, they set fire to the walls, and once the flames were out of control, they took off."

The friar interrupted himself for a moment, to kiss the wooden cross hanging from his neck. "We saved what we could, and the friars, except for us, went to live with the Indians, for greater security. And we are on our way to present to the Viceroy the evidence of the wrongs done us."

We retired to our bedroom, which was a bit of space in the shack, separated from the rest by a few straw mats suspended from the roof beams. It was teeming with cockroaches and other insects. My godfather was amazed at what the friars had told us. He said with certainty that the cause of their problems was the lack of a firm authority. We must make careful note of everything—not only to inform our superiors but also to determine to what point people who, by virtue of their family background and upbringing, ought to put into practice what they have been taught as faithful sons of the Church but nonetheless prove capable of turning into its persecutors when there is no one to make them obey and to punish their failings severely.

Along with that puzzling report, we had other news that encouraged us to carry on with our plans. The innkeeper told us that two individuals who fitted the descriptions of Rubén and Lucía, driving a packed mule, had come that way some twenty days before, heading east.

So we went on with our search, passing scattered villages and traversing great expanses of jungle. We saw what must have been the remains of the monastery that had burned down. All that was still standing was the framework of the tower, topped with a cross now turned to charcoal.

At one point we came across a man who, like Luengo the peddler, who visited our village, spent his time carting goods back and forth between various settlements and the coast. He rode on a big, dark-colored mule, very old and loaded with leather saddlebags as big as she was. In front of the saddlebags was a narrow saddle, where the peddler sat. Seen from a distance, the shape of the whole was quite strange. It looked like one of those great monstrous animals that, according to the tales people tell, live in isolated regions and sometimes lose their lives at the hands of knights-errant.

He welcomed our presence and spoke without a pause the whole time we kept each other company.

We passed many plots of ground that had been cultivated at one time or another but had once again been overgrown by the jungle. The reason why, the peddler said, was that the first breaking up of Indian communities had taken place in that region, in the days of the Adelantado don Francisco de Montejo, Sr., but pestilential fevers had killed off most of the people and forced the rest to abandon the land. He also said that such plagues, and others like it, had become common since the arrival of the conquistadors, and that they had decimated the Indian population.

He spoke hesitantly of the polemics between encomenderos and friars and there was merely a hint in what he said of a very mild criticism of the behavior of the encomenderos, for their ambition, he said, was no less than anybody else's. Knowing that they could not realize their ambitions by acquiring gold, they were eager to accumulate as quickly as possible whatever riches could be derived from the fruits of the earth. When my godfather expressed his surprise at the lukewarm reproaches he had leveled against the excesses of the encomenderos, the peddler burst out laughing.

"Sir," he said, "I am only a poor peddler who makes his living from the orders and errands of this person or that. It is not up to me to judge anyone's actions. But in their day those encomenderos were given license to settle in the Indies as persons worthy of complete confidence. Those who are now persecuting friars are longtime Christians, since, as you well know, no Lutheran, or Moor, or Jew, or convert, or gypsy is allowed to come to these lands."

On hearing those words, my godfather bowed his head and said nothing.

"To avoid entanglements with the Indians' ingenuousness, even lawyers are kept from coming to the Indies," the peddler added.

"That is only reasonable," my godfather said. "For even one, all by himself, would be capable of disturbing and upending the tranquillity of the Garden of Eden itself."

"But to return to what we were saying," the peddler went on, "the affliction of the encomenderos is understandably doubled, in view of the news making the rounds, to the effect that their grants of land and of Indian laborers are going to cease to be hereditary. Do you think that's reasonable?"

"I'm not the one to judge what His Majesty deems fitting to provide," my godfather replied curtly, thus bringing the discussion to a close.

At mid-afternoon, the merchant told us that, less than a league off, there was another village of friendly Indians where there was a Spaniard who had settled with a native family—a hospitable man who would be grateful for a visit from us and would give us shelter. We veered off in that direction, arriving in the village at sunset.

It turned out that the Spaniard had a talent for carving images, using different woods from the jungle. He made Virgin Marys, saints, and crucified Christs which he painted and which the peddler then undertook to distribute and sell.

He was an elderly man, and unlike the other people who travel these roads, who were always eager to learn what was happening on the other side of the ocean sea, or in the various provinces of the Indies, this man lacked that sort of curiosity.

When we explained the object of our search, the man assured us that two persons who fitted our description of them had passed by that way several days before:

a taciturn black man and an Indian girl, both of them Christians and both Spanish-speaking.

"What were they doing here?"

"They were in search of a party in which they said friends of theirs were traveling."

"We're those friends," my godfather said.

"I told them that no Christians had come this way for a long time. They then asked me if along some route that did not lead to the coast—a route which they must then follow—there was a village or settlement of Spaniards, and I informed them that four or five leagues north of here is the encomienda of don Antonio Martínez de Xaul. And that was where they headed."

Then he said something that left us both overjoyed: "There is no other road that leads to that encomienda except the one that passes through this village. Unless they headed for the coast by cutting through the jungle, which does not seem likely to me, they must be there still."

The man courteously invited us to stay for dinner, and we were served corn tortillas with stewed turkey and fruit. Afterward, we had a long conversation. At one point my godfather, who had been looking at the hand-carved statues, praised our host's talent and expressed surprise that he did not practice his art in a capital city, where he would doubtless enjoy public recognition and would be able to sell his works at a profit. The Spaniard replied that such things were of no interest to him.

"My dear friend," he said, "I have experienced that kind of life to the full, and I would not exchange a single moment of my peace in the depths of this jungle for all the years that I lived in the city in Castile. That was where I first engaged in this craft and where I endured scorn and pettiness and all that the envy of the mean-spirited brings with it. Like the notables of antiquity, today I hold the Court in contempt and sing the praises of rural life. And this jungle where the most beautiful birds take wing, and the most luxuriant and leafiest trees grow, and the brightest flowers and the sweetest fruits are to be found, is to me the best place on earth. I understand those ancient peoples who experienced time here as a fragment of eternity, for the last days of my life pass by in the same serenity."

The night was very mild and beyond the outside platform, where the glow from the long wax taper was growing dimmer and the dark of night beginning, the jungle was filled with murmurings. I took in his words as if they were my own, for that was the feeling I had experienced in the twins' village. But I said nothing.

My godfather, speaking slowly, said: "I understand your feelings and do not mean to reproach you for them. But it is my opinion that tranquillity of that sort is more suited to the Indian way of life and is one of the reasons for our victory over them. For we believe that the world is still waiting to be brought to perfection, which will come about only when the Kingdom of God has been realized, and to that end we must complete the evangelization of these unfortunates who believe that all is forever meant to be the way it is. We, dear friend, find it impossible to remain inactive."

The woodcarver sighed. "That is true. And as you

know, not only when it comes to Christianizing infidels, but also when it comes to filling one's pockets."

"The Holy Gospels are not against that," my godfather pointed out.

"Fortunately," the peddler asserted ironically. "For if filling one's pockets were not compatible with the spreading of the Kingdom of God, these Indians would go on being heathens for all the ages to come."

CHAPTER XIX

As we went on in the direction pointed out to us, the vegetation and the trees grew less dense. We came upon abandoned ruins, but they lacked the grandeur of those we had seen earlier.

On the first day, we did not pass a single dwelling or human being along the way, and that night slept on the ground, protected from wild animals by several bonfires, since during the day we had caught sight of at least one jaguar. On the second day, shortly after setting out, we saw a crudely carved stone cross on the edge of the path.

"We must be near Christians!" my godfather exclaimed.

It did not take us long to get there. A massive wooden gate decorated with interwoven tree branches marked the entrance. There were three Indians at the gate, wearing identical attire that surprised me—a dark-colored *huipil*, tied at the waist with a length of rope—and each of them carrying an harquebus. My godfather expressed his amazement in a loud voice. "Indians with harquebuses? I've never seen such a thing."

As we drew closer, the Indians came to meet us, and I could see that their harquebuses were only crude wooden imitations. The Indians greeted us in Castilian, asking the reason for our presence. We told them that we were looking for several persons who, according to a reliable source, might well be on the encomienda, and that we wished to speak with the encomendero.

The Indians asked us to wait in the shade of a small grove of trees. We could see that, along with these make-believe firearms, they had bows and arrows at the ready in a corner. One of the Indians went off down the foot-path at a run, while the others stood guard at the gate with the measured pace and the serious mien befitting soldiers on guard duty in an army camp.

In a short time a beardless young man arrived, with a sword at his waist. I deduced from his features that, like me, he must be the offspring of a Spaniard and an Indian. He greeted us with an exclamatory phrase in praise of Our Lord, which we answered with all due respect. Then my godfather explained the reason for our presence and he asked us to follow him, dismounted however, and bearing no other weapons save those at our waists. We climbed down from our mounts and tied our crossbows and quivers of arrows to their saddletrees, and led them by their halters.

A broad plain with crops of hemp, tomatoes, and beans, and orchards of avocado and papaya trees stretched before us as we made our way toward the village. Indians were laboring in the cultivated fields, and in the orchards and all around us there was evidence of intense human activity. Except for those engaged in actual physical effort, who wore only the traditional loincloth, the others were wearing the same long, dark-colored *huipil* tied at the waist with a length of rope, like a monk's habit.

The village was surrounded by a great palisade of tree trunks that leaned outward, with their tops hewn to a sharp point, in the manner of a military fortification. Along the palisade were several entry gates and we headed for the nearest one. There we were greeted affably, with phrases in praise of the Lord, by several Indians, who took our packed mounts from us, assuring us that they would be taken to our lodgings. Then the young man who had received us asked us to accompany him to the encomendero's residence. I noticed that almost all the Christians we met had the features of half-breeds.

The residence of don Antonio Martínez de Xaul, or Saul—I never did learn which—was one of four huts which, built in the center of the village, formed the arms of a cross.

Our escort spoke to a servant, who soon returned, asking us to follow him. We walked through the hut, whose cornice gleamed from much polishing, and out the back patio. The servant approached a man sitting on a bench who was milking a cow into a clay vessel, whispered something in his ear, and the man, after he had filled the vessel with milk, turned to us. He, too, was a mestizo.

"Praised be the Name of the Lord!" he intoned.

"May His Holy Name be forever praised," we countered.

"You arrived just as I was about to have my morning repast. Would you care to join me?"

We accepted, and after ordering that we be served, the encomendero washed his hands in a basin and led us to a lean-to, all twined with vines. It was cool and shady, and he bade us sit in the great leather chairs that filled the tiny room.

"I'm listening," he said, with a gesture of great deference.

My godfather told him briefly who we were and why we were in Yucatan, and then explained that we were in search of a servant of his, of the black race, and an Indian girl, one who was free—a member of our family—from whom we had been separated by a series of mischances. He said that once our party was reunited, we would continue our journey east to the coast, with the intent of boarding a ship en route to Panama, where we were to fill important posts in His Majesty's service.

The servant arrived with gourds in the form of bowls, filled with milk, fruit, and tortillas with honey, and the three of us ate with gusto.

My godfather then went on to say that, according to the latest reports—passed on to us by the Christian craftsman of images who lived in the Indian village to the south that was closest to the encomienda—the persons for whom we were searching had headed several days before in the direction of the encomienda. They had not returned by the trail leading to the village, apparently the only route connecting the encomienda and the main road that the Spaniards normally used to cross the peninsula.

"We wish, then, to find out whether they in fact arrived and are still here."

The encomendero summoned the servant and gave him instructions in a low voice. Then he addressed us with a satisfied gesture. "You will soon have news of them," he said.

He asked me most courteously whether, as my facial appearance indicated, I had Indian blood in my veins.

"Yes, certainly," I replied. "My father was Spanish, but my mother is a lady from Tlaxcala who married him after the conquest of México."

A short while later Lucía and Rubén arrived, and our reunion was a joyful one. We told them about the treachery of the bachelor-at-arms and my godfather's wound, and how he had finally been healed. Lucía told us how they, for their part, had gone searching from village to village, as we already knew, and that all the goods we had salvaged from the shipwreck were in good condition, as was the mule.

Once our embraces and explanations were over and done with, my godfather asked why they had stayed here for such a long time. For, even though it had fortunately led to our reunion, he could not help but be surprised to see both of them wearing the same long dark *huipil* as the rest of the inhabitants of the village.

Rubén and Lucía looked at each other and then at the

encomendero, who answered on their behalf. "It was my wish that they should remain for some time with me."

"Well, in any event, we shall now all leave together," my godfather said. "And the sooner the better."

"My good don Santiago, kindly lend an attentive ear to what I am about to tell you," the encomendero said. "Your departure cannot take place as quickly as all that. It is my intention to offer you my hospitality for several days and I cannot accept a refusal on your part."

The encomendero's manner was so affable and obliging that at no point did it cross our minds that he meant to keep us by force.

"But my lord don Antonio," my godfather said, "a murderous thief is at this very moment using my name, committing God only knows how many misdeeds."

"Don't let his head start trouble you," the encomendero said. "There is a shortcut from here to the eastern coast that can save you many days' journey on the main road. Moreover, the season is just beginning when the first ships put into port and stay there. You will have enough time to get your hands on him. But for now you will remain with me, and I will show you what, with the aid of the Lord our God, is being done in this territory. I also want you to meet Friar Laurentino, the saint who looks after the Lord's interests in this undertaking."

We were not able to converse longer with Lucía and Rubén, for they went off hurriedly at the pealing of a church bell. We were then accompanied to our quarters, in the immediate vicinity of the encomendero's hut. Before we went to bed, we noted that the entire village was under guard every hour of the day and night, like a military camp.

"This is a curious encomienda," my godfather said, "as curious as its encomendero. But we cannot violate such courtesy toward us."

My godfather thought that the encomendero's insistence was merely an indication of his generous hospitality and saw nothing strange in the behavior of Rubén and Lucía. I did not want to seem suspicious and said nothing, but the following day, when we were getting dressed, we discovered that my grandfather's sword and my poniard had disappeared.

My godfather uttered a few curses and went out into the street, where there were a number of soldiers, one of whom firmly requested that my godfather stay in the hut and not cause a commotion.

"I wish to see the encomendero," my godfather shouted. "I wish to see him this minute and hear from his own lips an explanation for this outrage."

"You will see him when the proper time comes. Wait now and keep calm."

They brought us a good breakfast, but my godfather refused even to taste it and remained lost in thought as I ate. Finally, one of the servants came to say that the encomendero awaited us.

CHAPTER XX

When we arrived at the encomendero's compound, the servants escorted us to the door of the same shack where we had been received the day before. The encomendero and a Franciscan friar were praying on their knees in the center of the room. Once they finished reciting their prayers, they crossed themselves and rose to their feet, and the encomendero don Antonio Martínez de Xaul—or Saul—came to welcome us with open arms.

"The peace of the Lord be with you," he said. "Did you have a good night's rest?"

My godfather answered very gruffly: "Sir, are you aware that we were stripped of our arms as we were sleeping, and that, when we asked to have them back this morning, your men detained us as though we were prisoners?"

With great emotion, don Antonio Martínez took him by both arms with his hands, giving signs of heartfelt feeling.

"I apologize, don Santiago. I am the cause of it all, but there is nothing about it that detracts from your honor or diminishes your freedom. Listen to me and then let us hear your opinion."

He bade us enter the shack. The Franciscan was a tall, slender man, with delicate, pale skin and bright blue eyes in which the morning light was reflected, illuminating his face with the air of exaltation found in certain images of saints.

"But first, allow me to introduce you to Friar Laurentino de la Urz, who is responsible for the religious administration of the encomienda."

My godfather's fury had not abated; he gave a slight nod of his head and stood there with his arms crossed. Without thinking, I kissed the rope belt around the friar's waist, as I would have kissed my teacher's.

"I pray you to sit down now and listen to what I am going to tell you," the encomendero said.

"I am quite comfortable the way I am," my godfather replied. "Speak, but by the grace of God my companions and I will leave here at noon today, with our supplies and our weapons."

"Your lordship don Santiago," don Antonio said, "in this encomienda the evangelization and instruction of the Indians is being carried out in such a way that it is a miracle. These people have become most devout and obedient to the law of God, and fine subjects of His Majesty. Harmony reigns between the one responsible for imparting Christ's doctrine and the one who organizes the work of these unfortunates. Are you not aware of the tensions and quarrels that exist elsewhere regarding such matters?"

"Some Franciscans we met on the road a few days ago told us that encomenderos had burned down their monastery," I said.

Don Antonio Martínez and the friar looked at each other, scandalized.

"May the Lord have mercy on us!" the encomendero exclaimed. "And how did such an abominable crime come about?"

I recounted what we had heard from the friars, after which don Antonio asserted, in a cutting voice: "That is proof of the necessity of rigorously pursuing my undertaking and makes my seeming discourtesy toward you all the more excusable. I want you to be witnesses for a time to what is taking place here and hope that if in the end, you do not wish to remain here and lend us a hand in our endeavors, you will at least be spokesmen for us and spread the news of our efforts."

He approached my godfather and said in a gentle voice: "I pray you to sit down, don Santiago. I beg you to trust me, if only for a short while."

My godfather looked at him sternly and did not reply, but he seated himself alongside him. Then all of us sat down and the encomendero went on talking.

"As you know, the encomiendas are granted by His Majesty for the purpose of inculcating in the Indians the truths of our faith and the grandeur of our country. We act as their guardians, helping them along the path to civilization. In exchange for such instruction, a portion of the fruits of their labor—which must be organized so as to be as efficient as possible—passes into the hands of those who devote themselves to the tasks of teaching and of organizing their work. However, as you also know, many abuses and even slavery are hidden beneath the outward manifestation of this ideal. There are a great many encomenderos who give no thought to evangelizing and teaching their Indians, only to reaping the greatest possible profit from them, even by resorting to the aid of a lash."

He fell silent, a pause that no one interrupted. He looked at each of us intently, and went on: "This encomienda is organized like a monastery. The prayers, the doctrine, the work assignments, and the instruction follow one upon the other according to a set of rules, which everyone follows. One-fifth of the profits from the Indians' labor is set apart, being owed, like all revenue, to His Majesty. But the remainder is used to augment the patrimony of the encomienda in order to improve the education of the Indians themselves, so that when they and their sons, and the sons of their sons, are civilized, they can continue to own their lands and be free subjects of the Crown."

There was another pause. Then the friar spoke. There was a metallic echo in his voice that went well with the gleam in his eyes.

"You must know, my sons, that it has never been as easy to attain the Kingdom of total charity as it is today.

The discovery of these lands, where so many hundreds of people who are humble and pure of heart—although until now in the grip of the devil—are awaiting their conversion to the true faith, is the sign from Providence that we are on the threshold of that millennium, which, as proclaimed in the Book of Saint John the Evangelist, is to precede the Last Judgment. And I believe that working for the attainment of the Kingdom is the finest of missions for any Christian."

The gestures of both the friar and don Antonio Martínez de Xaul—or Saul—were marked by those somewhat frenetic tremors that must cause prophets and saints to quake. I was impressed and scarcely dared breathe. As for my godfather, he, too, remained motionless in his folding chair, with crossed hands lying on his lap.

"It is necessary, however, to preserve in them whatever existed, before our arrival, that was innocent and good. That is why on this encomienda the true God is praised in the language of the Indians, and many of the feasts and forms of praise that were once meant to honor demons are used today to honor our Redeemer and his Virgin Mother."

"Trust in me, don Santiago," don Antonio Martínez persisted. "When you are thoroughly acquainted with our encomienda, leave when you feel the proper time has come, if that is your desire. But, meanwhile, keep your eyes open and take our words into consideration."

"And what about my sword?" my godfather exclaimed. "A sword is the mark of a soldier, as a cross is the mark of a man of the cloth."

"In the rule governing this community, only the guards

bear arms," don Antonio Martínez explained. "But I will have your arms returned to you if you so desire."

That was how the discussion ended, and my godfather and I took our leave. We had asked to speak with Lucía and were escorted to one of the large huts in which Indian girls, dressed in the now familiar dark-colored *huipil,* were weaving as they sang pious hymns. After a time Lucía came out and greeted us, although the presence of the other girls seemed to inhibit her. Then, when the weavers left their work to go somewhere else, I was able to exchange a few sentences freely with her.

"Why didn't you leave?"

"We weren't able to," she answered. "They kept delaying us day after day. We know now that nobody can leave here."

"How do you know that?"

"The Indians told me. They say that don Antonio and Friar Laurentino are good men, very good men. But that leaving is a mortal sin. Whoever escapes gets killed."

"Are you all right?"

"Yes. And much better now that I know you're still alive. I was afraid for you. I never liked that bachelor-at-arms."

We had to break off our conversation, for one of the Indian girls approached and spoke to her in the language of the region. Lucía went off, after embracing me and kissing my godfather's hand.

The next day, on learning that I knew how to write, the encomendero assigned me to the courtyard of the storehouses and supply rooms, where it would be my job to record the daily movement of provisions, seeds, tools, men, and domestic animals. As for my godfather, he was to act as the encomendero's counselor, even though my godfather would scarcely speak to him. They had given back my godfather's sword, but he was now accompanied by two of the mestizo aides of the encomendero's who, though they treated him with great courtesy, never left him by himself.

Among the subjects in which the male Indians were given instruction, I was able to see that they were being taught the arts of war, just as Spanish foot soldiers were. They marched about the countryside in unison, to the sounds of drums and trumpets like one of His Majesty's armies, and they learned to handle their wooden harquebuses, loading them, taking aim, and firing them as though they were real weapons. They were also learning to ride horseback, using the mounts of the encomienda and ours. They also engaged in long exercises that involved shooting arrows with their primitive bows but also practicing the use of crossbows.

I described all that to my godfather. His initial ill humor and indignation had now turned into a mixture of amazement and concern. Though religious by nature, he was tired of the many ceremonies he was obliged to attend every day, and also of the succession and frequency of prayers to be recited.

"This is a life fit for Carthusian monks!" he exclaimed.

I helped him to take off his boots, and afterward he sat there looking at the roof, where several of the birds that often entered the hut were fluttering about.

"Miguel," he finally said with a sigh, "I think we've fallen into the hands of a pair of fanatics. I am afraid, to tell the truth, it won't be easy for us to get out of here."

"But their plans appear to be in keeping with God's law and His Majesty's intentions."

"Including making horsemen of the Indians, and teaching them the skills of our infantrymen?" He sighed again. "Miguel, my son, you're still very young and don't yet know to what degree the road to hell is paved with good intentions. The bad encomenderos do violence to their Indians and rob them of the fruits of their labor, and even of their blood and their lives, with no attempt at concealment. But this man of good will, aided by a saintly friar, deprives those who are closest to him of their freedom and orders the lives of the others with drumrolls and the sounds of trumpets, from dawn to dark. And thus he does violence to one and all, even though his intentions are charitable. May God help us."

CHAPTER XXI

A week later, after High Mass on Sunday, my godfather—keeping his natural impatience in check—told don Antonio Martínez politely that he had the most favorable opinion of the evangelical and civic work that was being done on the encomienda, but that his personal commitments—including one that, as the encomendero himself knew, was concerned directly with his honor—did not allow him to delay his departure one minute more. He therefore requested that the animals and equipment that belonged to us be placed at our disposal and that he free Rubén and Lucía from their obligations, so that they might join us.

The encomendero listened attentively to my godfather's words and then, courteously and with placating gestures, said that he would keep them well in mind, that he would reflect seriously and we would soon know his answer, though he said we should remember that Rubén and Lucía were both performing important tasks as aides to Friar Laurentino, and that I, with my knowledge of writing and arithmetic, had made myself indispensable in the storehouses.

When we returned to our quarters, my godfather unburdened himself of his fury by shouting curses and lashing out at empty air with such strong punches that they would have broken a man's jaw had they landed on one.

Finally he calmed down and spoke to me in a stern, gloomy voice: "Miguel, we must make plans to escape from here. The longer we wait, the harder it will be for us to get away from this place, and the farther away that scoundrel of a bachelor-at-arms will be."

I agreed, and that very night we began to look into all possibilities. We discovered that the encomienda was, in fact, a solid fortification and that at night an even more careful watch was kept on the portcullises and palisades. The stables remained locked and guarded, and soldiers patrolled the streets of the village.

I moved about inconspicuously in the vicinity of our hut, observing when the sentries came to inspect the palisade and how often the guard changed. Someone on patrol saw my hulking body, and I was ordered to halt. I ran instead and they swiftly followed me. I even heard the whizz of crossbow darts above my head. I finally flung myself under a hut and managed to pass their meticulous inspection unperceived, though I returned to our quarters soaking wet and filthy from cattle dung.

On the following day, the encomendero summoned us and warned us, with his usual amiability but in a serious tone of voice, that we should not go out after dark. In view of the news of the uprisings in which the friars' monastery was burned down, he had ordered a curfew after the church bell rang for evening prayers. Anyone who violated the curfew did so at his own risk, running the danger of being wounded or killed by a sentry or a patrol.

My godfather and I were indignant. The encomendero was clearly not willing to let us go on our way. We both decided not to leave our quarters, and I spent the following morning setting down in writing this account of our misadventures, with new ink and paper that I took from the storehouse as payment, however meager, for my labors as scribe and bookkeeper.

At midday, instead of the servant who usually brought us the earthenware vessels with our meal, it was Lucía herself who came. She informed us that our attitude was of great concern to the friar, who bore us no ill will and who, having nothing at all to do with discipline, which was exclusively under the jurisdiction of the encomendero, feared that we would be punished severely, and begged us to be obedient.

"Let him dare try to punish us!" my godfather exclaimed, grasping the pommel of his sword in a rage. "If he has the audacity to make such a move, his troops will suddenly be fewer in number, and I may even reach the encomendero himself and cut off his ears."

But I knew how improbable it was that these threats could be carried out, for the encomendero had many men at his command, his village was an impregnable fortress, and we were far away, with regard both to distance and to the rate at which news travels, to be able to get any sort of help.

I then thought of something that I had completely forgotten. While my clothes dried after my nighttime scouting expedition, I took out of my bag a clean pair of breeches and a shirt, and along with my change of clothes, I took out the packet that the sorcerer in the twins' village had given me as a token of gratitude. The features of the two sisters suddenly flashed through my mind and it surprised me how effectively time blots out memories and the ache of a wound.

"Lucía," I said. "Can you speak with the chief of these Indians?"

"They belong to various groups, various families. There is more than one cacique," she replied. "There are two great caciques and three lesser ones."

"Can you speak with them?"

"Yes. I see them every day."

I handed her the packet wrapped in a kerchief that contained the pierced stone.

"Show them this. Tell them that I need their help, that we want to leave here."

I waited impatiently, but Lucía did not return that day and I could see that the door of our hut was heavily guarded. On the following day, our breakfast was brought to us by the usual servant, along with a young mestizo who acted as a lieutenant during armed encounters.

"Don Antonio is waiting for you," he said to me.

My godfather swiftly rose to his feet.

"Not you," the soldier said. "It's your godson he's waiting for."

My godfather and I looked at each other without a word.

"I'm coming," I answered.

I followed the lieutenant, leaving my godfather very worried. When I arrived at the encomendero's dwelling, I was taken aback by the scene that greeted my eyes. At the door, motionless and with their arms folded across their chests, were a number of Indians. They were not wearing long dark *huipiles*, however, but only their loincloths, and, around their necks, the necklaces and insignia of their rank. I realized that they were the caciques and was filled with curiosity.

The encomendero received me inside the dark hut. Temporarily blinded as I was after the intense sunlight outside, it took me a few moments to make out my surroundings. He was sitting behind a table covered in an Indian cloth, on which the kerchief and the piece of jade were placed.

"It would appear that you have great power, Miguel."

"I owe any power that may come to me through these objects to nothing save a faithful friendship."

He sat there looking at me for a few moments and then began to speak slowly. He said that because of the mixture of blood that ran through my veins, I ought to understand him and support his views. He recounted in detail his plans and his projects, which he said would be realized over the long term, so far in the future that by then we would all be dead.

Since I have no idea in whose hands this manuscript may end up, I am not going to reproduce his words literally, as they might be wrongly interpreted: for don Antonio Martínez de Saul (or Xaul), the half-breed son of a Castilian now dead and an Indian woman from La Española, felt intensely in his soul the suffering and the destruction of the Indians. He wanted—taking from the Spaniards whatever they had brought with them that was good—to regenerate the natives and instill in their centuries-old spirit new motivation for resisting the power of the Conquest to enslave, and to encourage them to survive, regaining in the future the glory they had lost.

I say that I am not reproducing his words literally, so as not to encourage wicked falsehoods: for the encomendero declared himself to be a faithful subject of His Majesty's and a devoted son of Holy Mother Church, and so his intentions seemed honorable. And I myself, imagining a future when the Indians, not having ceased to be themselves yet at the same time embodying what was good in the Spaniards, freely ruled their lives under the auspices of our King, was fascinated by the project and eager to help to see it come to fruition.

But I told the encomendero that, before making any decision, I had to accompany my godfather to find what was ours, which, if it were used by the malefactor who stole it from us, could become the basis of many wrongs and grave misdeeds.

"The tribal chieftains support you," he replied, with a spiteful air. "Be off with you as soon as possible."

I picked up the kerchief and the stone and quickly joined my godfather, giving him the good news. We sought out Lucía, who also rejoiced and busied herself gathering together our animals and our belongings. We were ready to leave before midmorning.

But Lucía spoke to me with a contrite air. "Miguel, there's a difficulty concerning Rubén."

"What is it?"

"He doesn't want to leave."

"I'll speak with him."

I accompanied Lucía to the hut next to the church, where the unmarried men had their quarters. Rubén was in the garden, looking sad.

"I don't want to leave this place, my lord," he said. "I want to stay here, with the brothers and Friar Laurentino, keeping the canonical hours and reciting the prayers."

I didn't know what to say and went back to my godfather. He was angry at the news. "So he doesn't want to come with us? I swear in God's name that if he doesn't go immediately to where the mules are, I'll drive him there with a whip."

"Godfather," I said, "he is determined to stay. It is my belief that you ought not force him to leave."

"He's my servant!" he said. "I raised him in my own house from the moment they brought him from Guinea, when he was just a little boy. I've treated him as one of the family. Is this his way of repaying me?"

"Let this be the price of our freedom, godfather, and let us depart," I said in reply.

He looked at me and snorted, pulling the last straps of his baldric taut. I went out into the street and a little later he came out and clapped me on the back.

"So be it," he said. "Furthermore, it would not be right

for us to force the will of someone who would gladly stay in this place that is partly a Carthusian monastery and partly a military barracks, requiring the same submissiveness as a sentence to the galleys."

We each mounted one of the three pack animals, between which we had divided the load. We left at midday, bidding no one farewell.

CHAPTER XXII

My godfather headed our group, silent and grim-faced, no doubt preoccupied by the thought of losing track of the man who had attacked us and stolen our name and money. Lucía and I followed him, each of us mounted on a mule, happy to be finally leaving together.

Lucía told me that, since the time we had gone off with the bachelor-at-arms and never come back, her entire will had been focused on finding us, to which purpose she had journeyed many leagues. She had seen the great disorder that held sway in the territory.

I in turn recounted our own adventures, more or less in detail, from the time we followed the bachelor until our reunion. I expressed my admiration for the way of life of the Indians we had come in contact with. She objected to some of my opinions, however.

"Despite all their wisdom, their infighting paved the way for the victory of the conquistadors," she said.

"They have lost almost all their grandeur," I said. "Haven't you seen the beautiful temples that they erected hundreds of years ago? The Indians are merely a shadow of what they once were."

"That's because they subjected their slaves to hard labor."

I burst out laughing. Lucía had been a servant since she was a child and is usually reserved regarding the merits and exploits of all peoples.

We stopped at the house of the Christian who carved religious images. He told us that it was eight or ten days' journey to the coast; that we should follow the road and not leave it. The road passed through the first territory to be claimed by the Spaniards and since then, had been conquered by the previous Adelantado, so it was thoroughly pacified and we could travel through it without fear of attack.

Once on the road, we asked about the bachelor-at-arms at all the villages and encomiendas we came to along our route. He was known everywhere and also feared—or so it seemed to us—and almost everyone confirmed that he had been seen sometime earlier, headed for the coast, in the company of his two servants.

We reached the coast eight days after leaving don Antonio Martínez's encomienda. There were buildings from a lovely ancient city still standing, built along tall cliffs that overlooked a bright blue sea and beaches of snow-white sands. The Indians had appropriately called it the City of Daybreak, as the sun turned it a gleaming gold from the moment it rose out of the ocean, endowing it with a singular splendor.

There were no longer any Indians in this city. One of the beaches was fitted out as a port, though it was difficult for boats, which come in only in dry weather, to reach. On the beach, in one of the ancient structures, was a military garrison, and around it a handful of huts which had been erected to serve as storehouses, an inn, and a couple of ships' chandlers.

At the garrison we returned the two mules we'd borrowed. We were told that the bachelor-at-arms and his servants had passed through and had embarked for Nombre de Dios in a brigantine carrying a load of salt. On hearing that news, my godfather was beside himself. He and I ran down to the beach, where there was a boat riding at anchor by a crude wharf made of tree trunks.

It was another brigantine and my godfather's spirits rose, only to fall again after a conversation with the captain.

The latter was a corpulent man with ruddy cheeks and a calm, quiet way of speaking. He listened to my godfather voice his desires to set out for Nombre de Dios as soon as possible, but he replied that, in fact, that was not his ship's destination. He said he was willing to change his course to Nombre de Dios, but—considering the cost of transporting the three of us, with our mounts and equipment—would do so only for a very large sum of money.

My godfather was bent on striking a deal with the

captain and controlled his temper, bargaining at length with him. Finally, the captain agreed to transport us for 165 pesos in pure gold. Obviously, such a sum was well beyond our means, which barely amounted to twenty pesos. Then my godfather took the Adelantado's letter out of his leather pouch and without a word handed it to the captain.

"What is this?" the captain asked.

"Read it," my godfather said. "You will then realize that you are not dealing with ordinary people and that our guarantors are very highly placed."

The captain read the letter to himself, his lips moving syllable by syllable. Finally he flung his arms wide open in a woebegone gesture.

"My esteemed sir," he said. "This proof would be more than enough and I would take you to the ends of the earth without asking for a single maravedí, if the decision were mine alone. But I own this ship in partnership with a man of the cloth who is a saint when it comes to that which is God's, and is equally rigorous when it comes to the business dealings of this world. In the contract establishing our partnership, it is specified that we will offer neither the transporting of cargo nor passage on credit, even if reimbursement is personally guaranteed by the Great Khan or the Emperor of the island of Trapobana."

My godfather grew red in the face and I grabbed him by one arm and gripped him firmly, as a sign to him to remain calm.

"Are you making mock of me?" he said to the captain.

"There is no mockery whatsoever intended sir," the

captain said. "I am unable to transport the three of you on these terms. I need cash in advance, or goods of like value. For twenty pesos, your mount with its trappings, and that sword of yours, I can offer passage to you alone, if you wish; but to transport the three of you and your animals I need at least the sum I mentioned."

"Transport me alone?" my godfather bristled. "There is no point in even discussing it."

"Look," the captain said. "Next to the garrison is a merchant who might loan you the money. I for my part, as I told you, have a partner who does not allow me to make such arrangements."

My godfather snorted indignantly. I tugged on his arm and made him step back.

"What is this merchant's name?" I asked the captain.

"I don't know," he said. "His nickname is Pins, but he doesn't like hearing himself called that. Ask the soldiers."

We went back to the garrison without a word and paid a visit to the commander, a veteran soldier. His face was horribly disfigured—a mark perhaps of an encounter in battle with the Indians, who were highly skillful at hurling stones and left many a Spaniard with a wound in the head or teeth missing. In general he had a very slovenly look about him.

He perused the letter from the Adelantado most carefully and then turned to my godfather. "It is not in my power to force the captain to give you passage. Nor can I help you out with my own money, inasmuch as I am much poorer than you, though in the very near future, thanks to a post as royal magistrate that my lord the Adelantado has promised me, I shall be out of the difficulties I am in," he said. "The man who is called Pins, Nicanor Tordesillas, is a suspicious and greedy sort. But doubtless he is the only person who can help you in your present straits."

The merchant lived in a shack surrounded by a barricade made of tree trunks. The yard was guarded by two mastiffs. We called out to an Indian woman who was kneeling in the doorway, slowly grinding something in a mortar. She raised her head and then rose to her feet and disappeared into the half shadow of the shack. Finally a very skinny man came out, dressed in a doublet and hose that, from where we stood, looked rumpled and threadbare.

"What is it you want?" he asked curtly.

"Are you Nicanor Tordesillas?" my godfather inquired.

"Who is it that is looking for him?"

"The Royal Tribunal of Panama," my godfather replied testily.

The man was silent, but immediately called the dogs, tied them up, and approached the grilled gate. "Come in," he said. "I'm the one you're looking for."

We approached the shadow of the house and my godfather handed the man the Adelantado's letter, which the merchant read, furtively shifting his gaze back and forth from the paper to our faces and our attire.

"But this missive is not addressed to me personally," he finally said, handing the document back.

"The captain of the brigantine that is anchored at the wharf and the commander of the garrison have told us that you are the only one that might be able to help us. The captain apparently has a partner who does not allow him to provide transportation on credit, and the commander lacks the authority to oblige him to do so."

"Esteemed sir," the man said, "I am merely a humble merchant and I do not have the means to enter into formalities as lengthy as are doubtless necessary to be reimbursed by the Royal Tribunal for any moneys that I might advance you. Moreover, 125 pesos in pure gold are a fortune that at the moment I do not even have."

"One hundred sixty-five," my godfather corrected him. "I beg you to do your best. When I take over my post, you will not regret having helped me, I assure you."

"Very well," the merchant replied. "I will go over my accounts and let you know by this afternoon whether I can be of help to you."

We went to have our midday repast and told Lucía the latest news of our negotiations. My godfather was very discouraged.

"That's what the word written and signed by an Adelantado of His Majesty's is worth today," he commented. "I never imagined that I would experience such a thing at the hands of people who are Spaniards and Catholics. Titles and noble status are measured only by money these days."

That afternoon Lucía and I accompanied my godfather on his second visit to the merchant. But the house was as tightly sealed as a mausoleum and the dogs, whose number had doubled, came to the grilled gate and barked furiously at us.

"Rogues and charlatans," my godfather muttered.

We each took him by one arm and the three of us went off in the direction of the sea, which at that hour glistened in the late-afternoon sun. We sat down in the sand, and from where we were, we could make out the wharf and, above it, the cliffs crowned by the noble blocks of carved stone of the ancient temples. It was a peaceful hour and the pitiless heat had subsided a little. There was no one around, and the brigantine, with its sails struck, looked like a toy ship floating in a pond.

"The days ahead will be full of hardships," my godfather said. "For we are as far from Panama as from our homes, and whatever route we take, if we must go overland, will be full of dangers and privations."

It occurred to me that we also had the option of going back to don Antonio Martínez's, or joining the Adelantado, or even my twin Indian friends, but I said nothing.

Lucía, however, had the same thought and expressed it aloud. "It is not necessary to take either of those dangerous routes. The Adelantado will gladly accept you in his army, just as don Antonio Martínez would be overjoyed to have us settle in his village. And according to what Miguel has told me, you could also accept the hospitality of those friendly Indians who saved your life."

But my godfather rejected these proposals. "I have not left behind the friendship and company of my friends and the care of my animals, my crops, and my orchards to waste my life in wars and illusions that have nothing to do with me. And don't forget about the scoundrel that stole my credentials and has them in his possession at this very moment."

Then Lucía said: "Listen to me. I have the solution to our problems."

CHAPTER XXIII

We both focused our attention on her.

"Miguel," Lucía went on. "Before leaving home, your mother gave me, in great secrecy, a jewel. She told me to guard it as a precious treasure, but at the same time not to hesitate to use it should the need arise."

She searched about in her clothes. My godfather listened in astonishment, but with a mixture of irritation and surprise I had guessed what she was referring to. She took out the little pouch and handed it to us.

"What jewel are you talking about, my girl?" my godfather asked.

He untied the pouch, and the emerald suddenly appeared in all its transparent brilliance.

"For the love of heaven!" my godfather exclaimed. "What is that?"

He examined it minutely and then looked at us in disbelief. "It's an emerald. The most beautiful emerald I have ever seen. And polished in a most wondrous manner. How did doña Teresa come by it?"

Lucía indicated by a gesture that she had no idea.

"But this stone is of incalculable value," my godfather said, almost to himself.

He kept the palm of his hand extended and the green-colored sphere resting in it shone like the evening star in a setting sun.

"A fortune. A fortune belonging to your family," he added, looking at me.

"Doña Teresa told me that we should make use of it, if the need arose," Lucía repeated.

"But have you any idea what it may be worth, my girl?"

"Godfather," I said, "perhaps that merchant with the dogs will agree to lend us the money if we leave him the emerald as security for the loan."

My godfather reflected for a few moments. "This stone is worth a thousand times that price," he said.

"We can ask him for more money," Lucía suggested.

"Let's go see him this minute," my godfather exclaimed, putting the emerald back in the pouch.

The sun had gone down by the time we arrived at the merchant's shack. The dogs came to the grilled gate and began to bark with a fury that the shadows of dusk seemed to intensify. There was a light glowing inside the shack and my godfather shouted at the top of his lungs, calling the merchant.

The silhouette of the Indian woman appeared in the doorway. "Go away, go away. My master isn't here. He has gone away."

"I haven't come to ask him for anything. I want to make him a business proposition."

"Go away," the Indian woman repeated emphatically.

"Tell him that I wish to show him a very valuable jewel."

The Indian woman went inside and shortly thereafter the spindly figure of the merchant appeared at the door.

"What do Your Graces want now?" he asked.

"To show you something that may be of interest to you," my godfather replied.

"I can't make any deals based on what we talked about this morning," the man stated brusquely.

"I haven't brought papers. I brought something the likes of which you have never set eyes on before."

The merchant came to the grilled gate, carrying a small lantern in one hand.

"What do you mean by that?" he said, once face to face with us.

The dogs had stopped barking, but they went on growling, their eyes fierce.

"Aren't you going to open the gate?" my godfather asked.

"You've come too late. Tell me what it is you want."

My godfather showed him the little pouch and then took out the emerald, which gleamed in the semidarkness.

"Do you know what this is?" he said.

He reached through the grille and brought the jewel up to the merchant's face. The merchant's eyes widened in surprise and he put out his hand to take the stone, but my godfather closed his fist and withdrew his arm.

"If you want to have a closer look at it, let us come in."

"It looks like an emerald," the merchant murmured.

"It is one."

Then, without another word, the merchant tied the dogs up and showed us inside the hut, where the feeble light of a lantern illuminated a jumble of baskets, bundles, and other objects. He went over to the lantern and stared at the emerald for a long time.

Finally, he gave a sigh. "It's quite true. I've never seen anything like it," he said, with obvious admiration.

"Very well, then," my godfather replied in a firm voice. "Since the document of don Francisco de Montejo, Adelantado of His Majesty, with his signature in full, his personal flourish underneath, and his seal, is apparently not sufficient guarantee for you, perhaps this stone will merit more confidence on your part."

"In your case," the man replied, "I shall try to collect the money you need and will keep careful watch over your jewel."

"I have gone over my accounts carefully and my needs are greater than I thought," my godfather replied. "I am now in need of more pesos."

The discussion went on until after midnight, but the merchant would offer a loan of no more than three hundred pure-gold pesos. My godfather argued insistently for a higher sum, but the merchant swore that three hundred pesos was the most money he could possibly raise in the brief time that remained before the brigantine set sail.

And so the terms were settled, and a document drawn up in which it was stipulated that Nicanor Tordesillas would keep the stone on deposit for two years, within which time my godfather was to pay him back the sum that had been lent him, along with a substantial interest payment for each month until then. The merchant forced my godfather to agree that, if he had not paid back the loan and the interest once the two years were up, the emerald would remain in the merchant's possession in exchange for the cancellation of the debt and the payment on his part of two hundred pesos more, which, added to the original loan, would add up to the sum of five hundred pure-gold pesos.

"You know that the stone is worth a great deal more," my godfather protested.

"I won't deny it," the merchant said. "But I can't tie up any more money than that, and nobody hereabouts can offer you any more than I have."

We didn't sleep a wink that night. Once the transaction had been concluded, my godfather ordered Lucía and me to return to the inn, settle accounts, get our equipment in order, load the mule, and head for the wharf. He for his part went off to the brigantine to make the final arrangements for our journey.

Lucía and I arrived at the ship at dawn, leading the packed mule by the halter. My godfather greeted us with loud shouts from the poop deck. The captain was at his side, the expression on his face sleepy and ill-humored.

"Come on, you young ones!" my godfather shouted. "We're sailing with the tide!"

Several sailors, looking sleepy too, took charge of the bundles, while others tied girths around the mule, and after hoisting it in the air, deposited it at one end of the deck, near the cages for the hens and for the rabbits. It must have been eight in the morning, more or less, when we weighed anchor and the seamen began rowing to get the brigantine off the beach.

A brigantine is a very small vessel and our accommodations turned out to be really uncomfortable. The captain ensured that Lucía, the only woman on board, was given private quarters, though they, too, must have been uncomfortable, surrounded as she was by crates of cargo tied down with rope. My godfather and I found a place for ourselves each night as best we could, but no matter where we slept, it was always noisy and foul-smelling.

Our food and drink and the fodder for our animals was included in the price of the passage. The water was fresh—the brigantine took it on just before we set sail—and the cook, a rather elderly sailor from Galicia, made delicious meals on the sand stove.

The sky is cloudless and the wind is blowing steadily from aft, so we are making great headway as we sail swiftly before the wind. I have taken advantage of our smooth sailing to get out my writing kit and go on setting down my account, which was interrupted when we left the village of the Indian twins, and was just barely taken up again in the encomienda of don Antonio Martínez de Saul, or Xaul. The crew, like sailors in general, knows nothing of the skills or arts of reading and writing, and looks upon me with respect.

My godfather often complains about journeys by sea.

"The sea again," he murmurs. "By God's will, may everything be well."

But I have no fear of the sea. After my first experience—at the beginning of which a bout of seasickness laid me low for three days—I am as pleased at skimming over the waves as I am at journeying via the paths and trails that lead overland. I even delight in the endless solitude, in which it is possible to imagine that nothing of what I think or remember really exists, that everything is a dream, that the worldly universe consists of an infinite quantity of water being traversed by a single ship, the one I am in, whose destiny is fraught with perils. How the whistling of the wind in the rigging pleases me, as complex and as varied as though it were blowing through a vast forest.

I am not afraid of the sea. On the contrary, I have had a fondness for it ever since I looked upon it for the first time as it crashed against the sands of the beach, echoing with that endless, deep-pitched, massive sound that resembles no other. And, for all its inconveniences and tribulations, life at sea is much to my liking: the maneuvers and work that attune the ship to the wind that moves it; the litanies and songs that all through the night indicate the time and the changing of the watches; the camaraderie necessitated by the limited space; and the sailors' amazing and sometimes terrifying tales of life at sea.

Today, the ninth day of our voyage, a seaman shouted down from the crow's nest that to our stern there is another ship that seems to be following our course. This, too, is a clear day and the wind most favorable, though lighter than on preceding days. I had already put away my writing kit—just the day before, I had finished briefly describing the events that had taken place until then—but the approaching sails gave me the idea of describing the sea, dark blue and suddenly spattered with patches of foam, and the sky, as uncluttered and resplendent as a length of newly dyed linen cloth.

By midmorning it was possible to make out the other ship perfectly. It is a very handsome caravel, no doubt recently painted and varnished, with all its canvas unfurled, even the main topsail and the sprit sail. A ship like that, driven before the wind, brings to mind the marvels that mankind with all its imperfections manages to produce. Everyone is gazing at the caravel in fascination, wondering what fate it holds in store.

I, too, had gone over to the gunwale and was admiring the handsome appearance of the ship, from which scarcely a dart's flight separated us, when a small white cloud suddenly appeared on its starboard side, near the prow. We then heard a whistling noise close by and the impact of a cannonball in the water only a short distance from our stern, which coincided with the echo of the detonation.

"They're shooting at us!" the boatswain shouted. "Everyone to general quarters!"

The captain was nearby and I saw him turn pale. As though it were a pennant, the caravel hoisted a golden chasuble on its foremast.

"It's El Pulido!" the captain shouted. "The Elegant Pirate!"

On the deck of the caravel, which is now quite close, there are dozens of men with blunderbusses and crossbows. From the crow's nest, one of its seamen is shouting to us through a leather megaphone.

"Lie to! Lie to!" he seems to be saying.

My godfather has come out on deck and approaches the captain.

I leave off writing.

CHAPTER XXIV

As I have put down in writing, of my own volition, the account of my adventures, I have not concerned myself with the way in which I have recorded events nor even how much time it has taken to do so. Whenever I had the opportunity, I would take out my writing instruments, file my pens to a fine point, shake the inkwell, and after finding a place on which to place the paper—at times, the writing kit itself, perched on my knees—I devoted myself to this labor unhurriedly and with no other concerns save to remove from the quill pen the little hairs that might smudge my writing. But today I am beginning my task in order to fulfill a serious promise, and I feel plagued by the fear of not having enough skill to accomplish it in a satisfactory manner.

It all started with the ship which, after launching a warning cannon shot, signaled us to haul down our sails. Like a lament, the captain uttered a name. My godfather went to him and asked him to explain. I stopped writing and set my writing kit aside.

The captain said that the Elegant Pirate was famous along those sea lanes, that in recent years he had wreaked havoc on ships carrying cargo to and from the Indies, invariably seizing the cargo for himself and often burning the ships he attacked and killing their crews.

My godfather was of a mind to load our culverins and have all of us arm ourselves to repel the attack, but the captain regarded himself as already defeated even before the fight had begun. "There are twice as many of them as there are of us, and they are men experienced in boarding enemy ships. If we try to resist, we shall all lose our lives. In such circumstances, the Elegant Pirate is implacable."

"We can't surrender without a fight!" my godfather shouted.

"My godfather is right," I said. "We can't let ourselves fall into his hands so easily."

"I am the master of this ship!" the captain answered, beside himself with fury. "There will be no resistance!"

Lucía joined us. "Don Santiago, Miguel," she said. "Let the captain take the lead in this matter. After all, the command of the ship is his responsibility."

We looked at her in annoyance and she pointed to the other ship, which was drawing closer and closer: dozens of armed men were leaning over the gunwale.

"What is more, our captain has reason on his side. Any resistance would be useless."

The captain had left us and was shouting orders to haul down the sails and slow down the headway that the brigantine was making. After a number of maneuvers, the other vessel brought its starboard side up next to our port side. Its gunwale was much higher than ours, and as it came to us, over a dozen seamen leaped onto our boat and lashed the two vessels together. Then a man who looked like their boatswain leaped onto our ship, too, followed by a gang of armed men. He ordered our captain to round up on deck the entire crew and any passengers.

The men from the caravel were dressed in bizarre attire: black caps and colored neckerchiefs, velvet doublets with silver buttons, striped hose. The boatswain wore gold bracelets on his bare arms, and his hair was twisted into corkscrew curls.

When we had all been rounded up, the man with the corkscrew curls addressed us from the forecastle deck of our brigantine. He spoke faulty Castilian, and had a strange accent.

"Greetings from Captain Fransuá Darcasón through his spokesman the boatswain, whose good friends call him Joyous Juanelo. This is an act of retaliation for war damages. Your vessel is now our prize and you are hostages. Any attempt to resist will be met by the death penalty. Now, anyone who has on him any kind of weapon, even if it be only a small pocket knife, will throw it down at his feet. You will then help us inspect the cargo."

"What flag are you flying?" my godfather asked in a loud voice. "To what war damages do you refer?"

There was a great silence and the man who said he went by the name of Joyous Juanelo looked at us with surprise. Then we heard a voice coming from the other ship. A man, the only glimpse of whom we could catch was a cap adorned with elegant plumes and the sleeves of a splendid doublet, spoke to us first in a foreign tongue and then in Spanish.

"Sir," he said, "I shall explain my flag and the war damages. But remain silent now and obey me, or by the Holy Shroud you will not leave that deck on your own two feet."

"Captain, as you call yourself," my godfather replied, unsheathing his sword, "come down here if your courage equals your arrogance, and give me those reasons one by one, in man-to-man combat with your sword in hand."

"I shall fight alongside him," I shouted, taking out the small dagger that I had with me.

"And I shall help them in any way I can!" Lucía exclaimed, placing herself at our side.

But this chance for a fight ended there and then, for the captain of our own ship, and several of his men flung themselves on us from behind, easily disarming us.

"Elegant Pirate, sir," our captain shouted, "these are not members of the crew but passengers. The entire crew is respectfully at your command."

"I will take your action and your words into account, captain," the Elegant Pirate replied. "Tie the gentleman, the lad, and the lass up good and tight now. And give me their equipment and belongings, along with documents that identify them."

The inspection of our ship lasted only a short time and

the best of the cargo was immediately transferred to the caravel, including the animals that had not yet been slaughtered for food, as well as our mule. The pirates uttered joyful exclamations in their language as they hoisted them aboard and I assumed that they were rejoicing over the prospect of fresh meat.

The boatswain of the pirate ship demanded of our captain that he collect all the gold, jewels, and money that we had with us and that he put all of it in a leather sack, which he did, including the gold with which we had paid for our passage.

Finally, the man who said his name was Joyous Juanelo addressed us once more from the forecastle of our ship. "Captain Fransuá Darcasón thanks the captain and his crew for their cooperation, and to show his appreciation he spares the life of each and every one of you, nor will the ship suffer reprisal. But you must wait for us to withdraw a goodly distance before making any attempt to continue on your way. As for the passengers, they are prisoners and will now be brought aboard our ship."

We were taken to the other vessel without overly gentle treatment. When the three of us were deposited on deck—a most spacious one—the Elegant Pirate spoke to us from the foredeck: "You men will be put in irons and imprisoned. The girl will become my personal servant."

My godfather and I were taken to the hold and put in chains. There were other prisoners in the darkness, for their shackles clanked when they moved. The putrid smell of the bilge permeated the air.

"Miguel," my godfather said. "Almost all the voyages I have ever made by sea have been unfortunate experiences. The first time I boarded a ship, when I was just a lad like you, I was shipwrecked on the shoals of Finisterre and my life was spared through a miracle; the second time, Barbary pirates set my ship on fire; when I came to the Indies, the ship's cargo was not properly loaded and we kept heeling, sailing for more than a month on the verge of foundering."

We tried to talk to the other prisoners, but a voice speaking bad Castilian sounded from the hatchway. "Silence. A chat down there earns a prisoner a flogging."

We fell silent, and despite the stench of the place, the lack of a bedroll, and the shackles restraining my ankles, I fell asleep out of sheer exhaustion.

My godfather awakened me. A dim light illuminated his face. Then I saw that a sailor was removing our leg irons.

"What's happening?" I asked.

"I don't know," my godfather said. "It seems that the captain of this ship wants to talk to us."

We went up to the main deck and then to the deckhouse. Night had fallen and the sky was full of stars. A brisk breeze was moving the ship forward, all of its canvas unfurled.

The sailor who had freed us said a few words outside the captain's cabin, which were answered from inside. Then the door opened and Lucía appeared. She came over to us and although her face was in shadow, her voice was calm.

"Don Santiago, Miguel," she murmured. "Are you all right?"

"We're all in one piece, thanks be to God, my girl," my godfather replied. "And how about you?"

"I'm all right, too," she answered. "Come in."

We followed her. The poop deck was very roomy and at the far end of it, grasping the tiller and surrounded by navigation instruments illuminated by two small lamps, the pilot looked like an image on a mysterious altar.

To one side of the poop deck there was a cabin closed off by curtains. Our equipment was stored there. I noticed then that Lucía was dressed in her best.

"The captain has invited us to dine with him and asks you to dress for the occasion, if you please."

My godfather shook his head. "The captain is inviting us to dine with him. The same man who, without right or reason, robbed us and imprisoned us. Is he a madman? Are you mad, my girl?"

"Don Santiago," Lucía said, "I beg you to do his bidding, and please don't take my words as an impudence. You know that I respect you, but I believe that our lives and even my honor depend on our cooperating with him. Moreover, you are no longer prisoners. Your chains have been removed permanently and from now on these will be your quarters."

My godfather lightly stroked Lucía's cheeks with one hand. "Lucía, my girl," he said. "if you ask it of me, I shall do it. I will wear my most elegant attire and dine with this captain as though he were King Arthur himself."

We tidied up and dressed to the nines as we had not done since leaving home. My godfather donned a black hat with gorgeous quetzal plumes. When we were ready, Lucía accompanied us to the door of the cabin, and after asking us to wait a moment, went in by herself. She came out again immediately, saying: "The captain prays you to enter his quarters."

We went in. Awaiting us was the same man we had seen from the deck of the brigantine. His attire was of the sort that princes wear. He was bareheaded and had long dark hair, but the hair on his head and on his beard both bore touches of gray.

My godfather and I removed our headgear.

"Come in, come in, my good don Santiago Ordás and you, Miguel Villacé. I bid you welcome."

He had us sit at a table laid unlike any that I have ever seen in my life. The tablecloth was of the finest linen, doubtless woven with bobbins and lacepoints, like those from countries on the other side of the ocean. The dishes and goblets were gold and the captain's goblet had adornments and precious inlaid stones suitable for a chalice.

"This is not an attempt to compensate for the tribulations that I have caused you," the captain said, "but rather to show you my appreciation and my intention to make your stay on my ship pleasant."

The dinner consisted of a series of excellent viands and fragrant wines, and at the door of the cabin a group of musicians played the cittern, the lute, and the flute and sang traditional Castilian songs and madrigals, as well as songs in other languages.

"I should tell you," the captain said, "that of all the things created by man, there is to me nothing greater than the writing of stories, be they moral apologues or fantastical tales, chronicles or histories, true or imaginary. When I capture a ship, I value the good books as much as the treasure, even if the treasure be as vast and as great a prize as that of the great Atabaliba, who is said to have filled an enormous room with gold, as high as his fingertips would reach, with his arm upraised."

And, in all truth, the captain's cabin had in its walls, fitted between the ribs of the ship's frame, a great many wooden planks, and on them, lined up in rows, were hundreds of books of all shapes and sizes.

"For the pleasure of reading, I have tried to learn a number of languages, Latin and Tuscan and English as well. I learned the Spanish language when I was a prisoner in Madrid with my good King don Francisco. I consider my imprisonment then, despite all its hardships, as time well spent, for it gave me the chance to read many fine tales written in your tongue."

"Are you acquainted with the adventures of don Amadís?" I asked.

"I am familiar with them, my boy, just as I am familiar with those of his son Esplandián, those of his grandson Lisuarte, and those of his great-grandson Amadís of Greece. For despite the fact that your King has forbidden such books to be brought to these lands, the eagerness of people to read them must be such that many barrels and casks, instead of containing the wines indicated on their labels, arrive here secretly filled to the brim with such fabulous stories."

The wine had loosened my tongue. "To me, there is no better book than the one about don Amadís of Gaul," I said.

The captain burst out laughing, rose to his feet, and went over to a shelf, from which he took a large volume. "It's good reading, true enough. But to me the most wondrous book in the world is this one, just recently come off the printer's press. It concerns the incredibly horrific life of the great Gargantua, the father of Pantagruel—both descended from the lineage of giants—written by the illustrious Alcofribas Nasier—a book in which good food and drink are celebrated, and every sort of hypocrisy is abominated."

He leafed through the book with a smile, put it back on the shelf, and returned to the table.

"But, besides these books written out of the sheer urging of the imagination, I must tell you that I also greatly esteem the chronicles of real events. In my line of work, I have come to possess many accounts of conquests and invasions of unknown territories. Thus," he added, pointing to me, "I have had the pleasure of reading the chronicle that this lad is promptly setting down as each of your adventures takes place, and I have taken a heartfelt liking to all of you."

I felt embarrassed.

"The felony of which you were victims at the hands of that bachelor-at-arms filled me with rage, and I, too, was amorously won over by the beautiful twin sisters. I have decided, therefore, not only to apologize for my behavior toward you but also to take you to Nombre de Dios. I will give you your freedom without asking for ransom, or any sum of money in return, except for the chronicle written by this lad, which shall remain my property, though in the time that elapses until we arrive at Nombre de Dios he must bring it up to date, recording the most recent events and all the incidents that are taking place at present."

My godfather and Lucía were looking at me attentively.

"I shall do so most willingly," I replied, "when you return my writing kit to me."

The captain let out another hearty peal of laughter. "It will be given back to you tomorrow, along with your other possessions. Sleep in peace now. May you all enjoy your night's rest."

CHAPTER XXV

The ship continued its swift, calm crossing. When we arose the following morning, we were told that the captain was waiting for us. We climbed the steps of the hatchway ladder leading to the poop deck and approached the door of his cabin, which occupied the entire deck. A sailor opened the door and showed us in.

With the tableware and tablecloth now removed, the massive table had been turned into a command post, covered with marine charts and a compass and other instruments. The captain rose to his feet and greeted us cordially. He then turned and picked up several items from the top of a large chest.

"Miguel, here is your writing kit and the part of your adventures that you have finished. With this wind, I am of the opinion that barely two days are left before we arrive at Nombre de Dios. I hope that you will be able to complete your account."

"I'll set to work this very minute."

A smile appeared on the captain's face. "Wait just a bit, because you may have other news to convey."

Then he handed my godfather a packet wrapped in linen. "This is for you."

My godfather undid the linen wrapping. "My credentials!"

"That's right, my good don Santiago. The credentials whose real owner I learned of, in fact, from the account written by your godson."

"How did you come by them?"

The captain bade us sit and sat down himself in his roomy armchair on the other side of the table.

"A few days ago we sighted a large ship which, like your own, was following the route to Darien. Its captain was too impetuous and daring; he underestimated his strength and attempted to do battle with us. We were obliged to board the ship by force. It then turned out that the main cargo was salt. I will spare you the rest of the details, though I will tell you that the old tub will never sail again. Among the passengers was a man, accompanied by two servants, who had these documents with him. I took him prisoner along with his servants, expecting that a person of such great importance would doubtless bring a good-sized ransom."

My godfather suddenly rose to his feet. "Is he aboard this very ship, then?"

"He's right here, yes."

"Sir," my godfather said gravely, "I have a great debt to settle with that man. I beg you to allow me to do so, by returning our swords to both of us."

The captain was silent for a few moments. "As I told you yesterday, your godson's account awakened in me a great sympathy for you. My position as the supreme commander of this ship permits me to prevent the outcome of your quarrel to depend on a duel."

He broke off to wipe his hands with a delicate handkerchief that he took from his sleeve. He then went on. "Moreover, by settling the quarrel myself, I am entering Miguel's account, as though I were the personification of fate itself or a player in the author's imagination. Can there be a more pleasing thing for an avid reader of fables and adventures such as myself?"

"What do you mean?" I asked.

He rose to his feet and headed for the door. "Follow me."

We went up onto the top of the weather deck and approached the rail.

"Look," he said.

The sun was blinding at first, but we finally made out what he wanted to show us: three bodies were suspended from the yard by ropes; they had been hanged.

"The end of the adventures of the traitorous bachelor-at-arms," the captain exclaimed in triumph. "Hanged with his servants aboard *The Indomitable*; justice meted out by Captain Fransuá Darcasón, whom the Spaniards call the Elegant Pirate—El Pulido."

I felt ill. I had the writing kit under my arm and suddenly it seemed to me too heavy to bear. I leaned on the ship's rail.

"What's the matter, my boy?" the captain asked.

"Sir," I answered, "I didn't wish them to meet such a terrible punishment."

"Even though they intended to kill you and your good godfather?"

"Sir," I explained, "I did not wish such a terrible punishment to be visited upon them by my hand."

"By your hand?" he asked, "Were you the one who gave the order?"

"I wrote down the story," I said. "You acted after you read it. I bear a certain responsibility for their deaths."

"Come, come!" he said, in a suddenly gloomy voice. "All the world has lost is three scoundrels of the worst kind, who if they had gone on living would have put more good people in danger. Moreover, do you think that writing is an innocent activity?"

I said nothing. The sight of the hanged men swaying back and forth with the tossing of the caravel had made my godfather and Lucía fall silent, too.

"Miguel," the captain went on, "no written words are innocent. The most truthful account of events reflects the bias of the person who records it. The adventures of don Amadís and his lineage extol chivalry, not the ecclesiastical courts, not the clergy, not the labors of the peasants. The most imaginative book that has ever existed down through the centuries, the one about the giant Gargantua, which I showed to you yesterday, claims as its one aim to give enjoyment to its readers, but the author immediately launches on a telling mockery of popes, academicians, and royal counselors."

He shook off a mote of dust from one sleeve. "You mustn't feel the slightest pang of guilt, though, for once they are written, stories expand beyond the limits their authors think they set for them and take on whatever dimensions their readers will accept or define for themselves."

Nonetheless, I spent the rest of the morning feeling glum and listless, my soul weighed down by the bodies of those three unfortunates, in whose purple faces was mirrored their horrendous punishment.

I learned at the first hour in the afternoon that the bodies of the three hanged men had been thrown overboard. A messenger sent by the captain informed me that we would probably arrive at Nombre de Dios within twenty-four hours, adding that the captain would not slow down the ship to allow me to finish my account. So I sat down at the end of the poop deck, so as to have enough light, and went on writing.

I have said before that the obligation to finish the account aroused scruples in me and a certain fear that I would not complete the task with the same ease as when I wrote only for myself.

Fears of this sort gave rise to hesitations and doubts that had not troubled me before and it took me some time to begin again. When I did so, night had fallen and I realized that I must take advantage of every available minute, for the captain seemingly has a strict sense of his commitments and he has promised to leave us at Nombre de Dios in return for my handing over to him my completed account.

And so I barely slept last night. Sitting next to the helmsman—a man with only one eye, whose face was marked by two slashes in the form of an X, and the little fingers of both hands missing—I wrote on without stopping, by the light of the two lamps.

I slept for a couple of hours just before dawn. At first light, the captain summoned us to his quarters.

"In my opinion, by mid-afternoon we will have sighted the coast of Darien," he said. "I shall cast anchor off Nombre de Dios and a longboat will take you there with your belongings. I want now to settle accounts. I am not in the habit of returning moneys earned in my dangerous occupation, but in this case I will make an exception. The money for your passage, which the captain of the brigantine extorted from you, belongs to me as payment for the crossing, for I will have taken you to your destination. From the moneys requisitioned from you by my boatswain and the sums you were robbed of by the bachelor-at-arms, which I seized, I will deduct the expenses involved in the execution and burial of the three men: ropes, sacks, and the labors of the hangmen, plus fifty percent, as a minimum profit in my undertaking. I am returning the remainder to you, including payment for your mule, which increased the provisions in my larder, and also what might be regarded as indemnity for certain annoyances caused you in the past."

He looked fixedly at me. "And your account?"

"I'm just finishing it, sir."

"I expect you to hand it over when we cast anchor off Nombre de Dios. That is your part of this bargain."

"I will do what I promised."

In the early hours of the afternoon we sighted land and the steady favorable wind brought us swiftly to it. The seamen say this is Darien, at the spot called Nombre de Dios. I thought Nombre de Dios was a city, or even a port, but this is only a long beach without a wharf or shelter; the only thing visible in the distance are a few tumble-down shacks. The seamen also say that it is an unhealthy place, teeming with fevers. There are no other ships at anchor.

My chronicle ends here. I have divided it into chapters and I am going to hand it over to the captain immediately. As one last favor, I am going to ask him if I may keep this writing kit.

EPILOGUE

My dear mother, with a good friar who will be leaving in a few days for México–Tenochtitlán, I am sending this letter to you with news of our whereabouts. Don Santiago, Lucía, and I are well and are together in Panama. Rubén stayed behind, in good health and of his own free will, as sacristan in the church of an encomienda in the territory of Yucatan. Our mules, unfortunately, were lost, as well as Godfather's two horses.

I hope that all of you—my esteemed grandfather, Luisilla and Consolación and Marcos, my sisters and brother, as well as our other relatives, friends, and neighbors—are in good health. I hope that Micaela's joints don't ache too badly and that the harvest has been abundant. I imagine that the brown cow must have calved by now and that good Francisquillo won't have forgotten to ask Juan Guerrero's son to give him the fishnets I lent him.

I can tell you that the journey to this territory has been perilous and full of unforeseen events, many of which placed us in great danger. But everything turned out well in the end, with no other mishaps but the loss of a fair amount of our money, of some of our equipment, and of the animals, as I have mentioned.

We initially set out from Villa Rica de la Vera Cruz in a boat that leaked, and by a miracle landed in territory belonging to the Maya nation. The war of conquest is still going on there and we witnessed many horrible things.

A man—may God forgive his misdeeds against us, as he has since died a most horrendous death—robbed us and tried to take our lives. My godfather and I became separated from Rubén and Lucía, and we all endured many hardships before we were reunited.

I can also tell you that the round stone, the one you gave Lucía for safekeeping, helped pay for our passage on another vessel when we hadn't a penny left. But the second voyage was no better than the first. We were taken prisoner by one of those pirate captains who prey on and plunder vessels en route to and from the Indies. Our lives were spared only because the pirate captain took a liking to the account of our voyage and adventures that I was engaged in writing, and we even recovered some of our money.

The pirate captain—a man with the manners and attire of a grand lord, though capable of great cruelty—in the end brought us to Nombre de Dios, and we were transported to shore in a small boat. Nombre de Dios is a particularly inhospitable place. Because of the unhealthy conditions, many men and animals have died this year, among them all the beasts of burden, and only after great effort did we succeed in finding some Indians who agreed to transport our belongings.

We made the journey from Nombre de Dios to Panama on foot, on a rough, winding road more than ten leagues long, which follows putrid streams and lakes swarming with mosquitoes. There were also poisonous reptiles and other predators.

Filthy and exhausted, but in good health, we finally reached Panama. Panama is a large city, with a good port and a fair number of houses built of stone and mortar. In the port there are quite a few vessels making for Peru, and it may soon be the right time to undertake such a journey.

We put up at a fine inn, and I give you my word, Mother, I had never before seen so many different dishes as those which were prepared in that hostelry, nor more comfortable rooms and beds. Many highly placed visitors stay there, with their servants and their retinues, and at night we heard fascinating stories about Peru, at present mired in a terrible struggle among the Spaniards. Before the conquest, Inca chieftains had had absolute power, governing their vast empire with great orderliness, and—so they say—even the humblest of their subjects never went hungry.

The day after our arrival, Godfather and I dressed in our best clothes from among those we still have left after so many vicissitudes, and headed, booted and hatted, with our swords at our waists, to the seat of the Royal

Tribunal. It was guarded by the first decently dressed Spanish soldiers I have seen since I left home, for those who are finishing up the job of pacifying Yucatan dress in the rags and makeshift clothes that are the usual attire of conquistadors in moments of hardship in the course of their undertakings.

Don Santiago intended to call on several of the Lord Justices in person, but, as it turned out, they were all busy attending to their offices or holding meetings that could not be interrupted. Don Santiago asked that a day be fixed for his audience, but they were unable to assign us a definite date.

We were finally received by a very thin man, dressed in black from head to foot, who turned out to be a court clerk of more or less high rank in those offices. He was going over a huge pile of dossiers and only when he had looked at all the documents and marked each page with a symbol did he address us.

I sensed that Godfather was on the point of showing his irritation, for you know him well and know that, while he is the kindliest man in the world, he cannot bear to be treated with disrespect. But the official finally set aside his work and invited us to sit down, questioning us as to the reasons for our presence.

Don Santiago took out his credentials most solemnly and handed them to the scribe, who studied them minutely and said that they were indeed authentic and accurate down to the last detail. However, His Excellency the president of the Tribunal, who had arrived from Spain months earlier, had since gone off to Peru, heading for the port of El Callao, followed by a flotilla carrying the majority of those who held posts and offices under his authority.

Our delay in arriving had been much longer than expected, even in view of conditions at sea and the difficulties of the overland routes.

The clerk—who after having a good look at my godfather's documents had abandoned his initial curtness and adopted a much more open and obsequious manner—asked us to wait. He left us in a room whose walls were lined with huge wooden cabinets full of packets of documents tied with red ribbons, and thick volumes bound in leather and parchment. When he returned, he had a more solemn, even a distressed, expression on his face.

After sitting down, he informed us that on the list of posts assigned or to be assigned when the president of the Tribunal arrived, the name of my esteemed godfather was not included. He said this omission might be due to some mistake, or possibly the appointment had been revoked, since so long a time had passed without my godfather's claiming the post, with no explanation for the delay.

My godfather was astounded. He began to recount in detail all the problems we had met with in the course of our journey, but the scribe motioned to him to stop—all that was of no importance now. He said the next step would be to consult the original documents of the appointment, which were in the possession of the president, who had taken them with him to Peru along with the other documents and instructions of His Majesty concerning his judicial powers in those lands.

There was, however, one way to verify the present

status of the affair, and that was to check whether the copies of the original documents bore any date that limited my godfather's appointment. But these copies, if such existed, were in all likelihood in the safekeeping of one of the chief secretaries of the Royal Tribunal, who at the moment was not in Panama and would not be back for two or three weeks.

The clerk told us not to worry; when the copy of the credentials turned up, as was to be expected, the matter would be resolved and my good godfather could take up his post—and at the same time be included at once on the list of those receiving salaries corresponding to His Majesty's posts and offices.

Our conversation was long and tedious, and my godfather explained to the clerk that he intended to appoint me as his secretary. The man then said that if I knew how to write, he could hire me as a scribe. What with the greed for gold and the many uprisings, which allowed the bold to prosper, everyone was going off to Peru, and there was a scarcity of people to copy and file the countless documents accumulating at the Royal Tribunal.

As for the pay, it would not be too small a sum and it would be paid promptly, for the vacancies that existed at that time made it possible to hire such employees without prior authorization from the Council, which is located in Spain.

We told him that we would think about his offer and give him an answer the next day. That night, after Godfather, Lucía, and I had talked things over, I decided to sign up as a scribe of the Royal Tribunal. The position would allow me to keep a close eye on the status of my godfather's appointment—which was our main concern—and at the same time learn something of the practices and customs of the Tribunal, as well as bring in a little money to increase what we had on hand, for the inn wasn't cheap and my godfather led the sort of life befitting the prestigious position he ought by all rights to occupy in society.

I began, then, to work at the Royal Tribunal, Mother dearest, and have had so much writing to do that I am weary of it, and have put in many an unbearably tedious hour.

The offices where I work handle business and financial activities which are regulated by the local government authorities—everything from issuing a license to engage in a gainful activity such as setting up an inn, to making cloth or growing silkworms, down to settling intestate inheritances of farms and houses. The paperwork is interminable, the court clerks few, and the way of doing things most peculiar. In my opinion, time is lost, and effort as well, in the filling out of documents that make no sense, though they may bear all the official stamps and seals and contain all the furthermores and whereases that you can imagine.

As it happened, two weeks went by, and then three, and the secretary in charge of the documents that might confirm my godfather's appointment fell ill, and we had to wait another two weeks before he took up his post again. And the secretary is an elderly man who is always in poor health, always in danger of contracting one of the fevers of this insalubrious place.

But when my godfather's claim could at last be looked

into, it turned out that there was among the secretary's archives no copy whatsoever of don Santiago's appointment. Moreover, even if such a copy existed and his right to the post was proven, there would still be a serious problem regarding the payment of his salary, for nowhere were the necessary credits approved and provided for, and though there was more than enough money to hire replacements for those who retired or dropped out of their jobs, there was no sum sufficient to cover the salary owed for discharging the duties of a post of such high standing.

The court clerk who had employed me blamed the situation—and the errors, omissions, misplacements of documents, and contradictions that regularly occurred—on the frequent changes that the manner of governing is subject to. He told me in confidence that he had been working in the Indies, in the offices of His Majesty—on the islands and on Terra Firma—for thirty-five years, and that he had seen in those who occupy the highest positions a hunger for power that leads them to make friends more readily than to do justice. The result is that people's wills become corrupted and what prevails in one and all is the sheer coveting of earthly goods.

We were finally able to arrange for the secretary in question to receive my godfather, but the meeting merely confirmed what we already knew. So, despite the fact that his credentials are legal, the signatures genuine, and all the documents properly drawn up, my godfather has no post.

In order to remedy the error, the secretary sees nothing else to do but to write to Spain with the request that the situation be rectified, or else seek out the president of the Royal Tribunal himself in Peru, so that he can bring his authority to bear to settle the matter.

You can imagine how gloomy we were, my godfather in particular, who had had so many hopes and dreams pinned on this post. But he forced himself to swallow his pride, and after calculating how much money we had left, we moved to another inn where the company is neither as distinguished nor the meals as delicious nor the bedrooms as spacious and clean.

There was a point, however, when we still had enough money to return home or set out for Peru, but we knew that if we waited much longer in Panama, with all the resulting expenses—despite the income from my work as a scribe, which in reality is meager—eventually it would be impossible to choose either alternative.

The three of us had a long talk. Lucía said she would abide by whatever decision we made, though she was in favor of our returning home. Despite the fact that we had managed to survive so many misfortunes, she said, there was no doubt that luck had hardly been favorable to us, and to persist in our plan would seem to be tempting fate. And if we spent our remaining funds on passage to Peru, where if don Santiago's claim was not honored—however just it undoubtedly is—we would find ourselves without money, amid the dangerous civil disorder that has broken out there.

I agreed with many of Lucía's arguments, Mother dearest, and aside from that, I am eager to embrace you, and my grandfather and brother and sisters and friends as well; but, on the other hand, it distressed me to see my godfather, after so much expense and so much effort, deprived of his post with neither an explanation nor an apology. This honor was freely granted him because of his fine reputation; he had never asked for it; and, moreover, there is no convincing proof whatever that it has been annulled or revoked.

I told him that I would gladly go along with whatever he decided, including accompanying him to Peru, where, despite all the disturbances, there is a chance that we can take part in some undertaking that will bring us honor and perhaps even profit.

But, as I have said, my godfather was very downcast. He said that taking off for Peru would be madness and that we three would do better to go back to our village while we still had the means to do so, since, when all was said and done, more was lost by that King don Rodrigo, because of whose stubborn love intrigues the Moors had invaded the Kingdoms of Spain.

But that night don Santiago had a dream. And even though, as you know, he looks down on any sort of superstition and does not believe in prophecies or premonitions of any kind, the dream left him uneasy and apprehensive.

In don Santiago's dream, according to the account he gave us the following day, he found himself in a place that was completely enclosed yet very spacious, which appeared to be the nave of a great church but was not one, since there were no saints or images or anything reminiscent of the sacred. Everything was dark and he found himself experiencing a great serenity, when a clear light began to dawn and he heard a voice. The clear light glowed green like the emerald you know, and then Godfather saw it, floating in the darkness like a propitious sign; the voice was very soft and gentle, a woman's voice that was pleasing to the ear. And as the stone glowed even more brightly, the voice told him that he should head for Peru without the slightest worry, for he would find justice there and he could do His Majesty great services. The voice kept repeating this message, until don Santiago woke up.

I repeat that the dream has left my godfather uneasy, and I think that in the end his inclination will be to undertake the voyage to Peru. I think that only the need to board a ship again keeps him from making up his mind.

Around the time of my esteemed godfather's dream, the friar whom I mentioned at the beginning of this letter arrived at our inn. Apparently His Majesty helps friars to travel with money from his royal treasury, and the amount a friar receives depends on which Order he belongs to. This friar is not one of the greatest beneficiaries, and since his Order does not have a monastery in Panama, he has taken up lodgings, as I have said, in the same hostelry where we have put up.

The friar knew about Godfather's problems and told him not to fret, for he had met people in Peru who had experienced similar misfortunes in the offices of the Royal Tribunal, and the president of the Tribunal had in all instances resolved their predicament once they had submitted a petition to him.

The friar also told us that Peru was in turmoil and that he had gone there to explore the possibility of founding a monastery for his Order. In the end, however, he decided to return to the newly built home monastery in México–Tenochtitlán.

As our village is located near the route he is taking from Veracruz, I asked him if it would be possible for him to deliver this letter, in view of the detour necessary to reach the village from the main road. He said that he would be happy to deliver it, and since then I have done nothing else in this inn, or at the office, but write this letter, despite the fact that I have many documents to copy.

What with the vivid images from his dream and the friar's descriptions as to how well disposed the president of the Tribunal is toward claims such as his, it would appear that my godfather will finally decide to embark for Peru. The weather is now favorable, and my godfather and Lucía have already investigated how much it costs for the transport of passengers and their goods.

If we end up shipping out from here, it will be very soon. I think of you often with my most heartfelt affection. I also remember with love my grandfather and my brother and sisters. Don Santiago sends you his most respectful regards and Lucía sends you an embrace, and asks you to embrace Luisilla, Consolación, and Micaela in her name. I will send you more news of us when I have the chance, if we have not returned home before then. I pray you receive all possible blessings.

Miguel